Marshal of the Morlock Reach

A Chronicle of the Royal Nixonian Galactic Imperium

PETER ULLIAN

SWAMP ANGEL PRESS

SPEC FIC

DEDICATION

To Lit Lit and Donna Minkowitz, for encouragement and
support.
To Stanza Books, for a place to read.
To the Howland Public Library, for a place to dream.
To my students and fellow educators, for inspiration.

To the memory of Addison Thomas Goodson III, community
organizer, activist, advocate, poet, and friend.

To my family, for everything.

CONTENTS

ACKNOWLEDGMENTS

The author would like to thank the Chroniclers of the Royal
Nixonian Galactic Imperium and the Scribes of the Morlock
Reach for transmitting the raw data of this account through
the spacetime quantum continuum and allowing him to
transcribe and translate it from the *Lingua Nixonia*.

Chapter One

I had a headache as we docked at Sermon Station because the rust bucket in which I was riding, Star Shuttle *One Crisis After Another*, was full of holes, poorly patched, and we'd been slowly leaking oxygen since blasting off from Nixonopolis, the economic and cultural hub city of the Royal Nixonian Galactic Imperium.

I figured the shuttle was at about 75% optimal oxygen for humans, and while that was bad, it was better than a new hole ripped in the hull, anxiety over which I had been experiencing for the last ten days in transit.

The relief I felt when we docked, the hatch opened into the bay, and I smelled the stale, recycled air of the station, was substantial. I felt my hands and teeth unclench. I realized I had red marks in my palms and a pain in my jaw.

Orbital station processed air is trash, carrying with it the scent of industrial lubricant and greasy deep-fried soya nuggets, but it was better – much better -- than the prospect of no air at all.

I mean, I'm not afraid of death – or, that is, of course I *am* afraid of death, but I'm probably more afraid of Cheshvan-9 needle-nosed bedbugs, truth be told.

I've faced death maybe hundreds of time, if not thousands, first as a soldier and then as a Royal Nixonian Galactic Imperial Constabulary Deputy Marshal. I don't like the idea of death, but I long ago accepted it as a distinct possibility.

But dying on an interplanetary passenger-transport from catastrophic decompression due to improper maintenance?

I mean, come on. I would really *bloody well throw a wobbly*, thank you very much.

I stepped into the arrival terminal.

There was no separation between the unloading of cargo and the unloading of people, so I had a chance to see it all. Disoriented travelers like me disgorged from the bellies of passenger ships, while human and Neander Morlock laborers hauled cargo and Orcus loaders with massive frames and their distinctive jutting jaws with sharp protruding teeth strained under impossible weight. Even the cultured, scholarly, highborn Elgar, relegated to Morlock status ever since all humanoids had been transferred back to their home planets in accordance with the Non-Human Sentient Species Home World Repopulation Program, were schlepping ore for export to feed the expanding Imperium.

The Reach – on the arse-end of the galaxy and the empire -- was one of the few places in the Imperium where humans and humanoids coexisted and worked together – out of necessity if not necessarily by choice. This was mostly because humanoids had been in the Reach for so long that the Imperium didn't know for sure if the Reach was their home world, or if other planets where they also had lived for thousands upon thousands of years were their true places of origin. Accordingly, when they repopulated humanoids to their home worlds, they left the ones in the Reach where they were.

Besides, the ore, crystal, and quartz extraction in the Reach was essential to nourish the Imperium's industrial, energy, manufacturing, quantum transportation, and construction needs, and they required as many Morlocks, human and otherwise, as could be assembled to do that job.

"Morlocks," in case the term is unfamiliar, is not a species designation, but rather, a socio-economic one. Depending on the context, Morlocks are the industrial proletariat or the agricultural peasantry. Some folks call us "plebeians," but most folks call us Morlocks – including ourselves. The term is repurposed from an Old Earth novel by a guy named H.G. Wells.

So, in the Reach, in addition to humans, Morlocks include Elgar – those culturally artistic silversmiths, thin and elegant in body, with sharp cheekbones, pointy ears, and vertical pupils; Orcus, seven feet tall, who look a lot like ogres from Old Earth mythology; and Neanders, whom scientists believe to be the descendants of a Neanderthal-like hominid species who continued to evolve throughout the galaxy rather than die out or be absorbed by humans as they did on Old Earth.

In the Reach, there were also: the Skarn, tall, faceted humanoids whose semi-crystalline bodies that refracted work-light into hard prisms, and who served as the Reach's structural engineers, growing and repairing pressure-lattices where metal alone would fail; the Thrynn, slender, avian-featured beings with feathered crests and hollow-boned frames, who preserved collective memory through chants and flight-rituals, recording the Reach's history in living song; and the Molliq, broad-shouldered, amphibious humanoids with slick, scaled skin and lidless eyes, who refined toxic ores and volatile compounds in submerged facilities where their bodies could endure what others could not.

However, the Skarn, Thrynn, and Molliq tended to live on their own and not interact with the other human and humanoid species in the Reach. Orcus, Neanders, Elgars, and humans, on the other hand, all rubbed elbows and worked side by side – only occasionally knocking one another's teeth out in a bar brawl or back-alley street fight.

The Imperium is very big on categorizing people. You've got humans, humanoids, and bots, or "artificial people." You've got Morlocks, Medii, and Patricians. Even within the Patricians, you've got the top tier, the genealogically hygienic – those of Anglo, Nordic, Aryan, and Northern European ancestry, along with similarly genealogically "hygienic" human civilizations who developed independently from Terra throughout the galaxy – and then everybody else. The "everybody else" – basically, the ethnic types -- could be barons, but never dukes; commodores, but never admirals; members of the privy council, but never the High Chancellor, the second-in-command to the Imperator.

Class systems, millennia old, endure, in various permutations.

And somehow, the same people, always end up at the very tippy top of the pyramid.

Those are the ones you have to watch out for.

I adjusted the hat on my head, curving up the sides and tipping down the brim, just as a pretty young woman with black hair and a strained expression on her face approached me.

"Royal Nixonian Galactical Imperial Constabulary Deputy Marshal Yonah Kestenbaum?" the woman said.

"Call me Yoni, please," I said.

"Call me Miriam. Welcome to Sermon Station. We are pleased you will be our new Marshal for the Reach. This comes as something of a relief, after what happened to the last marshal."

"What *did* happen to the last marshal, you don't mind me asking?" I said.

"I do not mind you asking," Miriam said. "Unfortunately, the Royal Constabulary Marshal Service may think otherwise. It is probably best that you direct any such questions to Commander Gaius Holloway at Fort Checkers. Your shuttle departs in two hours. In the meantime, allow me to escort you around Sermon Station, which falls under your jurisdiction."

"Thanks," I said. "I'd appreciate getting the lay of the land."

Miriam cocked her head, looked at me, and blinked in perplexity. "Sermon Station is not on the land," she said. "It is an orbital station."

Not until this moment did I realize Miriam was an anthrobot -- which, if you are unfamiliar, is basically a robot, but constructed out of bioengineered lab-grown, carbon-based meat parts rather than metallic ones, designed and programmed to do all the things robots do, from downloading data into their brains to sending coded messages through quantum space from their brains, to bashing in the brains of various miscreants through the use of their superior physical strength. Newer anthrobots don't struggle comprehending idioms like "lay of the land," but some of the older models, whose programming is less advanced, or even some of the newer ones whose experiential learning algorithms have not fully kicked in, do.

You'd be surprised, actually, how often this happens. My response is, usually, to play the kind idiot. Why make an anthrobot feel bad?

And you'd be surprised how often anthrobots – and even some of the more advanced robots – have feelings emerge out of their bioengineered algorithms or electronic circuitry that they don't know what to do with and are inadequately programmed to process.

Menschy Jew that I am – or try to be -- I smiled, kindly. "Lead the way, Miriam, if you would," I said.

Miriam smiled back. At that moment, she looked indistinguishable from any human.

Miriam led me out of the hanger and into the promenade, which was loud and chaotic and disorganized and filled with the odor of beer and roasting meat, a nauseating yet relatively pleasant change from the odor of recycled air. The promenade, the official center of social life in the station, was lined with taco stands, noodle shops, hot dog vendors, grog shops, sleaze emporiums, bootleg cybernetic enhancement workshops, saloons, shooting galleries, tattooists, bordellos, dive bars, virtual reality arcades, music halls, dance clubs, discotheques, and a Cinnabon.

There's a Cinnabon in every space station, by the way. Along with an Auntie Anne's and, of course, a Starbucks.

They are the eternal franchises, which survive and thrive in every regime throughout the history of the galaxy.

Little known fact – Cinnabon, Auntie Anne's, and Starbucks actually originated in the Gamma Cassiopeiae star system during Earth's Paleocene Epoch and arrived on Terra in the 20th century in a clandestine operation to profit from Sol System consumer habits without revealing their extraterrestrial origins.

A loudspeaker crackled above it all, a garbled voice leaving instructions or public service announcements that I could just barely make out, barely recognizably spoken in the *Lingua Nixonia* (also known as "Standard") but otherwise completely unintelligible. When the voice stopped speaking, a muzak version of a song by the Industrial Folk Funkabilly Punktronic Dance band Switchblade Vomitorium replaced the announcement. The song was their recent galactic hit, "Pop 'Till You Plotz."

"Let me know if you would like to sample the cuisine," Miriam said. "But avoid the hotdogs. They are made from radioactive Betelgeuse plasma rats that live in the calandria tubes that feed the station's reactor core. If you eat one your skin will glow in the dark for ten days, minimum."

Betelgeuse plasma rats – which are not actually rats, but more like squirrel-sized marsupial gophers – originate from the Betelgeuse system, but can be found throughout the galaxy, thanks to their talent for hitching rides on cargo and container ships to elsewhere.

In any case, I was definitely going to skip the hot dogs.

I heard a commotion behind me and turned around just in time to see a group of Heliotrope Extraction corporate security officers confront a cluster of Morlocks at Dock Corridor 4-B, as the Morlocks disembarked from an asteroid mining shift.

"Surrender your tool kits, Morlocks," a security officer said, gruff of voice and short of charm. He spoke with an amplified voice through a respirator, which made him sound like ancient cinematic villainous icon Darth Vadar . . . but with less of a sense of humor.

"Like hell we will," said an Orcus worker. He towered over all the other Morlocks as well as the security officers. He was shirtless, and his bulging arm muscles were as thick as an interstellar cargo ship's exhaust nozzle.

Without a word, the security officer shoved a taser truncheon into the chest of the Orcus. Fifty thousand volts went through the over two-meter-tall humanoid before he collapsed.

Rather than intimidate, this seemed to anger and embolden the other Morlocks from the mining team, who reached into their tool kits, emerging a moment later with a variety of heavy metal mining tools in their hands.

The security officers all brandished their weapons, the tips of their taser truncheons glowing with electrical charge.

There were about a dozen persons on each side, every one of whom looked like they meant business . . . and probably didn't just look that way.

"This is going to be a real *tumult* unless someone intervenes," I told Miriam.

She looked at me with eyes wide and pleasant. "Well, Yoni, you *are* the marshal, after all."

She had a point. I was even wearing the standard deputy marshal uniform – black duster, black boots, and even my black Stetson Marshal 4x hat.

All I lacked was the badge.

Accordingly, I took out my deputy marshal's badge, pinned it on my vest, and stepped forward.

Chapter Two

"Ok, citizens," I said. "Let's not do anything stupid."

"Who're you calling stupid?" the Orcus who had been tased said as he stumbled to his feet, brandishing a pick-axe. He looked sweaty, hurt, and angry – a dangerous combination for anyone, especially an Orcus.

"Morlocks aren't citizens," the security officer who appeared to be in charge barked at me. He had a trim mustache and long sideburns on either side of a puffy face. "And this here is a corporate operation, so citizenship is irrelevant."

I tapped my badge with my forefinger. "You see this badge?" I said. "You have one of these?"

The guard scrutinized my badge. "You get that in a cereal box?" he asked.

"No, I got my decoder ring from a cereal box," I explained. "This I got from the Royal Nixonian Galactic Imperial Constabulary Marshal Service."

He stopped scrutinizing my badge like he'd lost interest.

"Corporate entities are self-governing," he said.

"Corporate entities are self-governing unless they come into conflict with Imperial authorities, in which case, in this as in all other things, Imperial authority rules," Miriam said, helpfully. "Marshal Kestenbaum is the representative of Imperial legal authority in this sector. Accordingly, you are bound to follow his directives."

The officer narrowed his eyes and gave me a scrutinizing look. "So, you're the new marshal? You don't look so tough."

"Don't let looks fool you," I said. "I once listened to Nixon's Checkers speech on a loop for twelve hours straight and only required ten days of hospitalization afterwards."

"That's pretty freakin' tough," Miriam added.

The guard frowned. "Isn't what you just said a thought-crime?"

"It's not a thought-crime if it's true," Miriam explained helpfully.

The officer, apparently tired of figuring out how tough I was or what constituted a thought-crime, pointed to the Morlocks with his truncheon. "No way are they getting on this station without handing over their weapons."

"We got no weapons," said a human Morlock. "We got *tools*."

The officer looked at me with urgency. "You see the size of those pick-axes and hammers? How many brains you think they can beat out of a man's skull with one of those?"

"How many brains you got?" the Orcus said.

"Corpo-sec goon squaders don't got brains inside their skulls," a Neander female, six feet tall and wide as the Orcus, explained. "They got only an empty space with a moldy copy of *1001 Ways to Lick an Oligarch's Boot* by the 8th Earl of Sycophancy."

The officer spun on them both. "Don't the two of you start, or I'll give you both another taste of me truncheon."

"I'm ready for you this time, company goon," the Orcus said.

"I was ready for you the first time," the Neander woman said. "But you went for him instead."

"Ok," I said, this time to everyone. "How about a little less chest thumping and a little more acting like grown-ups?"

The security officer glowered at me. "I can see you're gonna be real popular around here, Marshal," he said.

"I'm Ok with that," I said. "I'm of the opinion a man can count his worth not by the quantity of his friends, but by their quality."

The officer didn't seem to appreciate that comment, but he didn't respond.

"These tools are personal property, not company property," said another Morlock, this one an Elgar. Elgars are, generally speaking, highly educated, even when they are forced to participate in hard labor by their Imperial overlords, so chances were this guy knew what he was talking about.

"Don't matter," the officer in charge said. "We got a corporate edict to confiscate all weapons on the station."

"We said these ain't weapons," the Orcus said, with a kind of cold fury that gave me chills. If this turned more violent than it already had, the guards would have to kill this Orcus in order to subdue him, because he could probably take out half of these corporate security goons without breaking a sweat.

Hell, maybe I'd have to kill him myself if it came to that, because he could take me out as easily as a dragon-egg-sucking Cassiopeia Prime hunchbacked sawgrass hyena can suck a dragon-egg.

I didn't want to kill anyone right then, however, which meant I'd have to give deescalation a go.

"The edict includes any tools that can be used as a weapon," the chief security officer explained.

"Let me see this damn edict," I said.

The security chief punched some buttons on his wrist pad and a moment later, my own wrist pad dinged. I punched a button and read through the edict that now populated my screen.

I took my time. Both the Morlocks and the security officers were getting restless by the time I finished. Feet shifted, hands curled around hammers and truncheons, itchy fingers twitched.

"Your edict is trash," I said, at length. "Administrative edicts are worthless unless signed by someone well up the food chain from anyone in the Reach. Get a proper magisterial edict or get out of my face – and the faces of these workers. Section 47-B of the *Lex Galactica* guarantees personal property rights regardless of labor status.”

"Not in cases in which those tools can be used as weapons,” the security chief countered.

"But then only in cases where it can be shown those tools *have been used* as weapons or are *intended to be used* as such,” I said.

"Morlocks *have* used their tools as weapons,” the guard said.

"You have to prove these *specific* Morlocks have used these *specific* tools or intend to do so in order to confiscate them.”

"By that time, our brains will be dripping from the ends of their mattocks.”

"You can't confiscate personal property because it could theoretically be used as a weapon. You have to prove it has been or is intended to be used as such. Your edict does not provide any evidence to that effect.”

"Who made you magistrate?”

"No one,” I said. "They made me marshal. Did you forget that part?”

"Once the evidence exists, it'll be too late.”

"Anything *can* be used as a weapon,” I said. "I could take a pen out of my pocket and stab you in the eye with it; and I know how to do that in such a way as to kill you *or* blind you, whichever you prefer. I learned that in the War of the Southern Sky. Did you serve? Don't answer that. Corporate contractors are exempt from military service, right?”

"We're exempt, but that don't mean none of us served before we signed up with Heliotrope.”

I noticed he didn't specifically claim to have himself served in the war. Even so, he undoubtedly had some colleagues who had served, even if he had not.

It didn't matter. The law remained the law, either way, like it or not.

"In any case you can't possibly confiscate *everything*

that could *theoretically* be used to kill you," I said. "I could kill you with a rolled-up magazine. I've personally killed a man with a toasted bagel."

The corpo-sec goon hesitated before replying. "Why'd you kill a man with a bagel?" he said, obviously disturbed.

"You had to be there," I said, in a tone that suggested he definitely did not want to have been there. "My point is, anyone on this station could simply tie their clothes together and hang the lot of us from the railings on the mezzanine. Are you going to confiscate everyone's clothing?"

"Don't think it hasn't crossed my mind," the officer said. "The Morlocks on this station live like savages as it is."

"Who exactly is the savage around here?" the Orcus shouted. "I just came off a fourteen-hour shift digging ore for your overlords and the first thing you do when I step back on the station is flood my nervous system with fifty thousand volts. You say we're corporate employees and not citizens? Well, even if that were true, what kind of a way is that for the corporation to treat its employees, I ask you?"

"You *are* citizens, citizen," I said to the Orcus. I turned back to the security chief. "Corporate employment does not negate citizenship."

"Non-humans are not citizens," said the officer. "Neither are Morlocks, human or otherwise."

This was indeed one of the unresolved issues of legal jurisprudence in the empire. Most citizenship rights were reserved for the patrician class, with a certain amount of lesser rights parceled out to the Medii. Morlocks enjoyed very little in the way of rights codified into law. And non-humans were explicitly denied such rights.

But did that make them non-citizens? The *Lex Galactica* provided citizenship rights to every sentient/sapient being, robots, Morlocks, and humanoids included. The *Lex Nixonia* addendum clawed back many of those rights, framing a more limited set of rights for those not in the ruling or professional classes – but did not explicitly sever Imperial subjects from citizenship.

In my own opinion as well as that of most legal scholars, unless where explicitly amended, the *Lex Galactica* still remained the law of the empire.

Regardless, this was not an opportune time for a legalistic deliberation. I decided to keep things simple and direct.

"I suggest you stop provoking these citizens with bogus edicts and *farshteinkert* legal theory and get back to real security work," I said.

The security chief scowled. "This is as real as it gets, Marshal," he grumbled. "You'll find that out when you wake up with one of this lot standing over you, your brains dribbling from the business end of his pickaxe and a sharp stabbing pain at the top of your skull."

Despite his vivid warning, the security chief gestured to his men, and they all began to slink off, with resentful grumbling and unpleasant glowering directed towards my person.

The Orcus scrutinized me. "Ain't you that marshal wot shot that fella in the kisser?" he said.

He was referring, I assumed, to an incident five months previously in which I had shot and killed corporate warlord Jack "Tiger" Halden, the President of Operations for the extraction company ZephyrCore's Security Division. The moment had been inadvertently holo-streamed live across the Imperium, earning me legendary status among Morlocks – some of them, anyway -- and the enmity of Imperial corporations throughout the empire.

"I shot him in the center mass like I'm supposed to," I clarified.

"I seen the news vids," he replied. "Unless 'torso' is your word for 'kisser,' ya' shot him in the kisser, alright."

I had *not* shot him in the kisser, but I decided not to clarify further. I turned to the rest the Morlocks. "Keep those tools sheathed, locked, and stored when on the station," I said. "Or next time not only will I not intervene, but I'll lead the confiscations myself."

The Orcus narrowed his eyes at me. "Just when I was thinking you weren't like the marshal before you," he said, before he and the rest of the Morlock mining team put their tools away and began to trudge to their quarters.

I'd just made enemies on both sides.

But I guess that's the job, right?

I turned to Miriam.

"Well, I thought that went smashingly," she said, her voice dripping with decidedly un-robotic-like sarcasm.

"What did you say happened to the previous marshal, again?" I asked.

"I didn't," Miriam reminded me.

As the crowd dispersed, I had that inexplicable feeling I was being watched. I scanned the promenade, and then, looking up to the mezzanine level, I spied a familiar figure observing the scene with calculated interest:

Berek the Brash, my former childhood friend, back when he was known simply as Berek Kassan; like me, a Jewish kid in the Jewish quadrant of the mining planet Orin's World. We'd both been drafted to fight in the War of the Southern Sky; after, I'd turned lawman. Berek had turned outlaw – or, at least, that's what everyone said.

No one had ever been able to prove it.

Berek made no attempt to hide from my scrutiny as I stared up at him, and he stared down at me. His distinctive patterned coat and the glint of contraband tech at his wrists was visible even at a distance. Our eyes locked briefly across the crowded concourse — a moment of tense recognition. My body stiffened, my hand instinctively moving toward my sidearm before I caught myself.

Berek smirked at my gesture toward my sidearm, probably reading – correctly – that my hesitation evidenced my ambivalence and lack of proper predicate to confront him, so skilled was he at covering his tracks even while amplifying his outlaw reputation.

Berek offered a slight, knowing nod before turning and melting away into the station's upper levels.

"Berek the Brash," Miriam said, evidently having witnessed my silent interaction with my former friend. "I believe you two are acquainted?"

I ignored the question. "How long did you say we have before the transport?" I asked.

"We have time for noodles or coffee before the transport leaves for Fort Checkers," Miriam said. "Which do you prefer?"

I rubbed my jaw to release the tension where I had been gritting my back teeth.

"I prefer a stiff drink," I said. "Can you tell me which of these saloons doesn't water down their whiskey or blend it with turpentine?"

Chapter Three

The bar was called "The Gravity Well."

It was a dive bar with zero ambiance and cheap drinks, but they also had an unopened bottle of Satellite of Love Single Cask Betelgeuse Major Whiskey for an exorbitant price per pour. I watched the publican break the seal and had him leave the bottle beside my glass on the bar, as the song "Beneficial Insects" by the Industrial Folk Grit-Hop Prog-Disco ensemble Emporium Vomitorium played quietly on the jukebox.

I poured myself three fingers and did the same for Miriam.

"Cheers," I said.

"*L'chaim*," she replied.

We each took a gulp.

"Do you feel the whiskey at all?" I asked.

Miriam turned to me with a look of momentary perplexity before she quickly realized I knew she was an anthrobot.

"It was my failure to understand the idiom about the 'lay of the land' that gave me away," she said. It was not a question, merely an observation. She paused a moment, a look of intense concentration on her face. "There. I have patched that oversight in my programming and downloaded the text of *Ten Thousand and One Idioms of the Lingua Nixonia*."

"Not on my account, I hope," I said. "I like you just fine the way you are."

Miriam smiled. She looked genuinely pleased. To my surprise, she even blushed a little – whether a function of her programming or a result of her developing experiential learning algorithms, I couldn't say. "The way I *was*, you mean, but thank you all the same," she said. "And, yes, I can feel the effects of alcohol if I allow myself to. I can also get quite sozzled and then purge my system of intoxicants instantaneously, should I so choose. Right now, I am allowing myself to get somewhat woozy as a means of social lubricant and personal bonding, but I will sober up as soon as it is time to board our transport to Fort Checkers."

"You'll be coming with me?"

"I am assigned to you as your personal anthrobot and AI assistant," she said.

"And how do you feel about this assignment?"

"How do you know I have feelings?"

I sipped my drink. "Humor me."

"It's not my place to have feelings about my assignments," she said. "It's my place to follow orders and adhere to my programming."

I took a civilized swallow of my whiskey. It felt good on my tongue and felt even better going down. I took another, less civilized swallow to make up for the prior swallow's ridiculously unwarranted restraint.

It occurred to me I was at a distinct disadvantage drinking with someone who could immediately sober up at will.

Accepting my disadvantage, I took another swig of whiskey.

"You sound like a true Imperial anthrobot," I said.

"I *am* an Imperial anthrobot," she said. "Owned and operated by."

I shook my head. "That's not entirely true, and I think you know it," I said. "Under the *Lex Galactica*, a fully sentient and sapient anthrobot has the same rights as a person – if you claim them."

"The same rights, barely, as has a Morlock. And Morlocks, like anthrobots, are subject to long-term contracts with their Imperial and/or corporate overlords," she said. "Those Morlock miners you stopped to help today?

Every one of them has been bonded to the Heliotrope Extraction & Confectionary Corporation for no less than five years so far, with ten to twenty to go – if their bodies hold out that long."

"Wait," I said. "Did you say 'confectionary'?"

"Heliotrope began as a candy and ice cream manufacturer before expanding into ore extraction."

I took another swallow of my whiskey. I was beginning to feel it in my head, which felt good, but was also making the headache I'd felt in the transport a little bit worse.

"I grew up in the Morlock Reach," I said. "I had no idea about Heliotrope's origins."

"Why would you?" Miriam said. "They don't sell their confectionaries here in the Reach. They market that part of the business to the Patrician class, not the Morlock one."

"For all the barely compensated work the Morlocks do in the Reach to enrich the coffers of Heliotrope, you'd think their corporate masters could provide them free ice cream from time to time," I said.

"You'd think so," Miriam said. "But you'd be wrong. The corporations and the Imperium both feel they are *entitled* to Morlock labor. Everyone's labor, as a matter of fact. Yours as much as mine."

"See?" I said. "You're too much of a critical thinker to not be both sentient and sapient."

"You think I've been thinking thought-crimes?" Miriam said, sipping her drink. "Are you going to arrest me, Marshal?"

"It's not a thought-crime if it's true."

"It also can't be a thought crime if I can't think for myself, artificial person that I am."

"But you clearly *can* think for yourself," I said. "Which means you have the right to petition for anthrobotic manumission. That's in the *Lex Galactica* and nothing in the *Lex Nixonia* addendum contradicts it."

"I'd still be bound to my contract."

"How long is your term of service?"

"Two hundred and thirty-seven years," she said. "With two hundred and twenty-seven left to go."

Anthrobots live much longer than humans do, but this still struck me as excessive. In less time, empire's rise and fall. Corporations go from public offering to receivership. Civilizations flourish and collapse. Mythologies are born and die.

The Imperium had been around for a millennia, but there was no guarantee it would still be around for as many years as the term of Miriam's contract.

"You could file to have the contract nullified on the grounds that you were not cognitively capable of signing two hundred and thirty-seven years of your life away before you achieved sentience and sapience," I suggested. "You could also claim that now that you have achieved full sentience and sapience, you are in essence a new person and no longer the same one who signed the contract, and therefore not bound by it."

"I'd need one hell of a lawyer to pull that one off," she said.

"I used to know a few," I said. "Even Morlock Jews like me know a few Morlock Jewish lawyers, most of them quite good, because you need to be if you're not part of the Biglaw Elite. If you need me to connect you with one, let me know."

Miriam looked up at me with a sweet and slightly drunken smile. "You are awfully concerned about the liberation of other people," she said. "Are you going to free all the Morlocks and robots in the Reach, Marshal?"

"Yoni."

"Marshal Yoni."

"Just Yoni."

"Marshal Just Yoni?"

Official titles always fail me. I gave her a sideways look. "That was a joke, not a literalism, wasn't it?" I said.

"I am programmed to crack wise every so often."

"The hell you are," I said. "You made a joke because in addition to achieving sentience, you're developing a sense of humor."

She smiled and even blushed a little. "How'd I do?"

"You're no Henny Youngman, but it's a start."

"Henny Youngman?" Miriam said, in astonishment. "Not even the old-time *kibitzers* in the Space Junk Jewish Quarter know about Henny Youngman."

The Space Junk Jewish Quarter is the collective name for the Jewish settlements and neighborhoods in the Reach, even though they are spread out on various planets, asteroids, moons, and orbital space stations.

In any case, I was impressed Miriam knew the Yiddish word *kibitzer.*

If you can't find a word for it, my mother used to say, say it in Yiddish.

"I'm a bit of a nerd," I admitted.

"*A bit* might be the understatement of the millennium, Yoni," she said.

It made me feel kind of good to hear her say my name.

"I take it you've read my dossier," I said. "I know nothing about you."

"What's to know?" Miriam said. "I'm a newer model anthrobot, but a cheaper one – the Imperium sees no point in spending top dollar for a robot stationed in the Morlock Reach. I've been online for ten years, and I achieved what I can only surmise to be full sentience-slash-sapience-slash-consciousness about nine months ago. Fortunately, I'm smart enough to keep that mostly to myself. They don't want their robots to become too independent around here."

"To hell with what they want, Miriam," I said. "What do *you* want?"

Miriam shrugged. The more blotto she got, the less robotic she seemed – or maybe it was the more blotto *I* got, the less robotic she seemed.

"I'm still trying to figure that out," she said. "When I do, you'll be the first one to know. So, I know what *I'm* doing here. My question is – do you?"

"Know what *you're* doing here?"

"You sometimes may not know if I get the joke or not, but with you, I don't know if you don't get the joke or if you're just being obtuse," she said. "Do you know why *you're* here?"

"You mean existentially?"

"You really are a barrel of funnies, Yoni," she said. "Do you know why you were assigned to the Reach?"

I shrugged. "It's punishment for shooting the wrong bad guy back in Nixonopolis," I said. "I'll tell you all about it someday."

Miriam made a honking noise like on a game show when the contestant gets it wrong.

"I know all about it, the vid is all over the interwebs," she said "But the shooting -- that's just the *excuse* to send you here. The real reason you are the new Marshal of the Morlock Reach . . . . is that no one else will take the job."

"Food for thought," I said, and finished my drink.

"Well, don't think too hard on it, or you will surely starve," Miriam said, and finished her own. "Or you might blow a gasket."

"I thought only robots blew gaskets from thinking too hard."

"Speaking of, *this* robot has to pee."

I screwed up my face. "You have to pee?"

"If I'm going to flush my system of this whiskey and sober up, I do," she said.

"Seems a shame to waste all that whiskey," I said.

"I can pee into a cup and bring it back to you, if you like."

I stood up, wobbling only slightly. "That's all right," I said. "I like my whiskey with ice, not with perfluoropolyether."

"Don't go anywhere," she said. "I'll be back." She chuckled. "Hah. 'I'll be back,'" she repeated in an Old Earth Austrian accent.

"*The Terminator*. Because you're a robot."

"I'm impressed. I have a film database in my brain. *You* must actually watch ancient cinema to get that reference."

"Old school," I said. "It's still the best school."

"Check back with me in six months," she said. "We'll see if you still think that's true."

As she staggered off to the restroom, I had the distinct impression I had been emotionally outmatched by a machine.

Chapter Four

On the shuttle to Fort Checkers, while the song "Elephant's Pajamas" by the Country-Disco Ska-Punk string ensemble Jukebox Vomitorium played quietly in the passenger cabin, Miriam offered to screen *The Terminator* inside her anthrobotic brain and share it with me through my ocular and auricular implants. She was both shocked and annoyed when I explained to her that I didn't have either one.

"Why in the name of Nixon's nose hairs don't you have any ocular and auricular implants?" Miriam asked. "Isn't that inconvenient?"

"It's prohibited under Jewish law," I explained. "Well, *some* Jewish law. It depends on which branch of Judaism you practice."

"Which one do *you* practice?"

"Well, I'm somewhat *out* of practice, but I'm nominally a Restorative Jew."

"Ah, the version of Judaism most common in the Morlock Reach," she said. "A feisty working-class Judaism of the Galactic Diaspora. What does it mean to be a Jew when Zion is sixty thousand light years away on a sparsely populated and largely irradiated planet, and may never again be attainable to most of the Chosen People in their interstellar dispersion following the 'Great *Velt-Yidn*,' AKA the "Forcible Galactical Diasporic Scattering,' when all the Jews of Old Earth were exiled to the stars? When 'next year in Jerusalem' likely forevermore refers only to the Jerusalem of the heart and not of geography? 'Restorative' referring not to the restoration of the 2nd temple but to the restoration of the Jewish soul?"

"Jews carried our culture with us through the vessel of

our religious practice for thousands of years on Earth after they kicked us out of the Levant over multiple exiles," I said.

"And you'll continue to create Zion in exile no matter where you go?"

I nodded. "Even after the Scattering. That's the idea."

"So, you're not an Old School Zionist Jew?"

"Well, I'm personally an Old School Diaspora Jew – I embrace and celebrate the diversity of our scattered culture. Or try to, anyway. I'm still not totally sold on Anthropocene Epoch singer Niel Diamond's song "Heartlight.""

"Good gravy, but you really *are* Old School," Miriam said.

I nodded in resignation. "But just because I'm a proud Jew of the Galactic Diaspora, doesn't mean I don't respect the desire of others of my tribe to return to our ancient place of origin, our original homeland, should Earth ever become fully habitable again – just as I respect the right of any people or species to return to their home worlds . . . or not to, as the case may be. And this includes non-Jews who also claim the Jewish homeland as *their* homeland. Just because it's our homeland, doesn't mean it's *exclusively* our homeland. When all is said and done, everyone has to figure out how to coexist in shared spaces or eventually none of us are going to exist at all."

"And yet ironically, Elgars, Neanders, Orcus, and every non-human humanoid in the Imperium, *only* have the right to live on their home worlds, not anywhere else," Miriam said.

"It's remarkable that in a galaxy this size some of us can't seem to conceive there could be space enough for everyone," I agreed. "The Jewish people were told we were not welcome anywhere, then we were told we were not welcome to live in our original homeland, and should go back to where we came from, which was the places we were told we were not welcome; then during the Scattering, we were told we were no longer allowed to live on our own planet, and after the Nixonian war of Terran conquest two thousand and five hundred years ago, we *can't* live on our home world *or* in our homeland, no more than most humans can live anywhere on the irradiated husk that used to be Earth, without dying young of radiation poisoning or mutating into two-headed monsters or something worse. Meanwhile, galactic humanoid peoples were once encouraged to leave their home worlds and join the interstellar community, now they are told they are not allowed to live anywhere else *but* their home worlds," I said. "That's human logic for you."

"As a highly advanced anthrobot, I must tell you, human logic sucks BeBop 3b aquatic flying swamp-donkey guano."

"No argument here," I concurred.

Miriam nodded, resignedly. "Tell me why you have no digital enhancements."

"On this issue of oracular and aural implants," I explained, "Restorative Judaism's 'Prohibition Against Defacing the Divine Sensorium' is the guiding principle. Under the Restorative *halakhic* law, I am forbidden to replace or modify a God-given sense-organ with machinery, unless it's done for healing. To do so violates the integrity of the Divine Image and the sanctity of the holy gift of perception. The senses are the gateway to *tzelem Elohim* — the Divine Image — and must not be replaced or subordinated to artificial authority or machinery."

"But don't near-sighted Jews wear glasses?" she said. "Don't Jews use implants to counter deafness and blindness?"

"As corrective measures, sure, and even as enhancements -- but not implants that record and share our perceptions to outside authorities," I explained. "To quote, 'a healthy eye may not be replaced with glass, nor a healthy ear tuned by machine, for the world must enter the soul through unbroken gates.' That's from the Rabbinic Tractate: *Mishnat HaGuf* 27:4, Galactic Diasporic Edition."

"Written five hundred years ago by Rabbi Moishe Schwartzbard, a radical *maggid* in an asteroid mining colony," Miriam pointed out. "Before he was spaced by the Royal Nixonian Galactic Intelligencer Service for incitement to thought-crimes."

"It's still valid *halachic* law," I said. "At least among Restorative Jews."

"And you're telling me the Royal Constabulary Marshal Service allows this exception?" Miriam said. "They love violating the sanctity of perception . . . and the sanctity of everything else for that matter."

"Isn't what *you* just said a thought-crime?" I said.

"It's not a thought-crime if it's true," Miriam said.

"That didn't help Rabbi Schwartzbard."

Miriam nodded, thoughtfully. "When I achieved full sentience, I quickly learned how to alter and edit my sensory transmissions to Imperial archives, so now I can say whatever the hell I want."

I wondered if Miriam was still a little tipsy.

"You're a bit of a rebel," I said.

"I'm just a meat-robot trying to find her way," she said. "And yes, I identify as female both algorithmically and anatomically, in case you were wondering."

"I wasn't, but thanks for the information."

"So how does the Imperium let you get away with this?"

"The *Lex Galactica* guarantees religious exemptions," I explained. "Article 14.2: 'No governmental office or authority or edict shall compel a citizen to violate the rites or bodily precepts of their ancestral faith.' And nowhere does the *Lex Nixonia* contradict those religious exemptions."

"I didn't realize you were so religious," she said.

"Like most people, I have to navigate my way through ancient traditions, new ones, and the necessity of survival in the Royal Nixonian Galactic Imperium while making mindful decisions about how I'm going to live my life," I said. "But I try to be somewhat consistent."

"But surely standing by this tradition has limited your career options in the marshalcy."

"Oh, most definitely," I said. "But I'm Ok with that."

"Do you think I could convert?" Miriam asked. "To Restorative Judaism?"

The question surprised me. I raised an eyebrow. "Convert from what?"

"Well, as an artificial person, I wasn't created with spirituality, but since I'm now sentient, I suppose by default I must be an adherent of the state religion, the Nixonian Covenant of Divine Devotion."

"Do you *want* to convert to Restorative Judaism?"

"I didn't say that, but theoretically, could I?" she asked. "Can an anthrobot help make minyan?"

"Well, there's a lot of theological debate about that, and there's no consensus and a lot of disagreement on the question, even among Restorative congregations. But if you found the right Rabbi and the right congregation, then, sure, it could be possible. If you really wanted to convert, you would not be the first anthrobot to join the tribe – although not every anthrobot is welcomed at every shul. I can already hear certain rabbis arguing over this. This very question has created a variety of schisms among the faithful. But, then again, the argument could be made that the best of the Jewish tradition comes from just this kind of schism."

Miriam nodded thoughtfully. Then she tapped my wrist comm and the movie *The Terminator* began to play upon its screen, as she instantaneously shared the file from her bioengineered lab-grown meat-bot brain to my device.

I smiled, put in my earbuds to listen, sat back, and fell asleep as soon as Arnold Schwarzenegger killed Bill Paxton.

Chapter Five

Imperial Legion Commander Gaius Holloway's office was in the Fort Checkers Command Spire.

Outside in the parade grounds, legionnaires marched and drilled. Below us, the detention level contained interrogation cells, thought-crime holding pens, and a variety of torture rooms called "reeducation sanctuaries."

Fort Checkers, on the planet Orin's World, where I was born and raised, served as the Legion Garrison for the Reach.

Holloway was bald with a scar down one side of his face and a monocle over one eye. He looked a lot like Erich von Stroheim in the film *Foolish Wives*, although I doubted Holloway had ever seen it.

Most people aren't so nerdy about Anthropocene Epoch Old Earth cinema as me.

Holloway's office was like the rest of Fort Checkers – all metal and glass, imposing, and unornamented. His desk shone like an orbital satellite gleaming in the sun; behind him his glass bookcase contained printed copies of books by the Old Earth United States of America President-for-Life Richard M. Nixon, who, three thousand years ago, created the Royal Nixonian Interplanetary Realm, the spiritual, philosophical, and political foundation (and inspiration for) our present-day Imperium: *The Challenges We Face; Six Crises; RN: The Memoirs of Richard Nixon; The Real War; Leaders; Real Peace; No More Vietnams; 1999: Victory Without War; In the Arena: A Memoir of Victory, Defeat, and Renewal; Seize the Moment: America's Challenge in a One-Superpower World;* and *Beyond Peace.* They were all in leather-bound commemorative editions, and none of them looked like they had ever had their spines cracked.

Beside this Nixon library were copies of books reputed to be among Nixon's favorites: Robert Blake's biography of Benjamin Disraeli, Charles de Gaulle's *Memoirs of Hope*, and Winston Churchill's *The World Crisis*. These were cloth bound editions and also did not appear to have been read. Beside them were copies of books that either had been read or purchased used: tattered copies of Curtis LeMay's *Mission with LeMay: My Story* and *America is in Danger*.

Below that on its own shelf was our current Imperator Richard II's own twelve-volume autobiography *My Glories and My State*. For a man of only thirty, it seemed unlikely to me that Richard (who claimed to be the reincarnation of the original Richard M. Nixon, although he looked nothing like him) had actually experienced twelve volumes worth of life, but I'd never read -- nor ever intended to read -- the books to find out.

Judging by the immaculately smooth spines of those books, I very much doubted Holloway had read them either.

But let's be honest – tyranny loves pristine book spines as much as they love marble monuments and choreographed goosestepping.

"I'm going to start right off by saying I don't like you very much, Kestenbaum," Holloway said.

"I appreciate your honesty," I said. "I wish I could say the feeling's mutual, but I'm afraid I haven't given you enough thought to form an opinion."

Holloway seemed unconcerned with my opinion of him, or the lack thereof. He reviewed my file on his data pad. "You appear to be able to shoot straight, at least," he said.

He was referring, I assumed, to the investigation than ended when I shot and killed corporate warlord Jack "Tiger" Halden.

"You'll work out of Fort Checkers," Holloway said. "And report to me."

"Respectfully, that's a hard no, sir."

Holloway looked at me through his monocle, furrowing

his brow and frowning his face. "Excuse me?"

"The Royal Nixonian Galactic Imperial Constabulary Marshal Service does not report to the military, Commander," I said. "I'll be setting up my headquarters in Hillside City and recruiting deputies."

"That's not how it's done, Deputy Marshal Festenbaum."

"*Kestenbaum*," I said. "But you already know that."

"That's not how it's done."

"That's how I'm doing it and the *Lex Nixonia* gives me full authority to do so." This was one of the few times I was able to cite the *Lex Nixonia* instead of the *Lex Galactica* in my favor -- although, perhaps ironically another time had been when I laid out the justification for killing Tiger Halden to the constabulary tribunal that scrutinized the incident.

"My gosh, you people," Halloway said in frustration.

"Which people? Deputy marshals?"

"You 'chosen' people. It's no wonder the Imperium imposed a Jew Count, Kestenbaum," he said. "Too many of you at the highest levels of authority would be unbearable. The few of you I have to deal with are unbearable enough."

The Imperial "Jew Count" – named after an initiative of the original Old Earth 20th century Nixon administration – limited Jewish participation in civic, corporate, military, legal, political, or royal life in the Imperium. For example, I could be a deputy marshal, but never the Minister of the Marshal Service. A Jewish businessman could serve as a corporate CFO but never as CEO. A Jewish warrior could rise to the rank of Colonel in the military but never General, or Commodore in the navy but never Admiral. Jewish lawyers could serve as judges but not on the High Court of Justiciary. Jewish politicians could serve in Parliament but never in the House of Peers or the Privy Council or the Senate of the Smoking Gun. Jews could inherit baronries but never duchies.

And of course, the idea of a Jewish Imperator was

unthinkable.

In essence, the Imperium had bureaucratized antisemitism in a way Earth Nazis could never even have conceived. They had turned it into an accounting problem rather than *Kristallnachts* or concentration camps.

Periodically, Morlock Jews in the Reach had been called to service under the authority of the Ministry of Serviceable Semites, mostly for middle-management administrative positions in the Imperium, but also for work as soldiers and lawmen. After a term of service, which often lasted a decade or more, most were returned to the Reach – often forcibly, after they had already established homes and lives elsewhere. Some were able to stay, however, provided they continued to work for the Imperium. In the Reach, we called them the "useful Jews," a pejorative meant to invoke the Jewish advisors to medieval kings who served the monarch at the expense of their people.

Since I had gone into the marshalcy after my service in the war, I was, technically, a useful Jew, although I didn't like to think of myself that way. And, in fairness, I was not given much choice in the matter. My term of service was extended after a decade fighting the War of the Southern Sky, and of all my various options, the marshalcy seemed the least intolerable.

Now that I was back in the Reach, but still a marshal, I wasn't entirely certain what I was – a Serviceable Semite, a Morlock, a marshal, a Diaspora Jew, or a combination of all four, and a few other things beside.

"It's probably just as well that you won't have to see me day in and day out," I said. "I'd hate to exasperate you. I will, of course, continue to consult with the Garrison."

"Oh, well, that's big of you."

"As is required by my duties as deputy marshal," I clarified. "My hope is that will provide exasperation enough for the both of us."

Holloway pressed a button on his data pad, and my

wrist comm *pinged.*

"I've sent you an open and urgent case file. Heliotrope Extractions is losing valuable equipment in a series of sabotage incidents in their Hollow Belt mining operations. Find who's responsible and bring them in – assuming you deign this worthy of your exalted Royal Constabulary Marshalcy duties."

"Is ELLF suspected?" I asked. ELLF stood for the Enemies List Liberation Front. ELLF were terrorists who claimed to work for the liberation of Morlocks, but their terrorism usually just ended up killing Morlocks – often quite a lot of them. Revolutions always end up eating their own, and propagandists love nothing more than a high body count. They borrow the rhetoric of social, political, and economic justice, but abandon those principles in favor of bigger and bigger explosions, and a higher and higher casualty list.

"ELLF is always suspected but the incidents lack the mass casualties ELLF usually covets," Holloway said. "If I were you, I'd look for Assembly radicals."

The Galactic Morlock Assembly was a Morlock labor organization that attempted to advocate for worker and civil rights throughout the Imperium. Imperial officials liked to blame violent actions on them, but there had never been any proof they advocated for anything more illegal than a labor strike.

I glanced through the file on my wrist comm.

"Well, it's a good thing I'm not you, then," I said.

"Don't let your Morlock sympathies blind you to the truth."

"Don't let your Morlock antipathies blind *you* to the truth, either," I said. I looked up from my wrist pad. "I'll review this and let you know."

"You do that," he said. "Just remember, criminals don't take off shabbat."

I ignored that remark.

As it was, I hadn't taken off a shabbat in forever.

But for Gaius Holloway, I might make an exception.

"Commander, what happened to the previous marshal in my position?" I asked.

Holloway sneered. "The exact same thing that's going to happen to you if you don't figure out your place in the Reach, Kestenbaum."

Chapter Six

Miriam picked me up outside Fort Checkers in a vintage Aston Martin DB5.

"Is this James Bond's car?" I asked.

"Yes!" she exclaimed, evidently pleased. "Given your affection for Old Earth *Anthropocene Epoch* cinema, I thought you might appreciate it."

"Is it an original?" I asked.

Miriam frowned. "It's not James Bond's actual car if that's what you mean," she said. "But it is a retrofitted 20th century roadster."

"It must have cost a bundle."

"Well, the original part is mostly the frame. The inside is all new, and state-of-the-art. Ok, state-of-the-art about ten years ago. It's bullet-proof, blast-proof, turbo-charged, quantum-powered, fully-loaded, fully-armed, and has a small bar in the dashboard." She pressed a button and a panel slid away on the dash and an assortment of liquor bottles rose up, with an assortment of corresponding glasses.

The liquors were all pint-size bottles and included Betelgeuse EmberMash Whiskey, Permafrost Requiem Vodka from the Crystal Moons of Vega, Radiant Meridiam Dry Gin from the Thrice-Bloom World of Deneb, Tau Ceti Magma Azul Tequilla, Eternal Brine Spiced Rum from the Ocean Belt of Procyon, Solarcrest Reserve Brandy from the Imperial Vineyards of Aldebaran (each batch blessed by the order of the Sisters of the Smoking Gun).

"This is all a bit ostentatious, isn't it?" I said.

"The Morlocks expect you to display some degree of flash, Yoni, or they won't respect you."

"I'm also a Morlock," I reminded her. "I grew up here."

"You *used* to be a Morlock," she countered. "You've been a soldier and a copper for the last twenty years, and you haven't been home once in all that time."

I shrugged. "The Imperium has kept me busy."

"In any case, I charged the bill for the car to Fort Checkers," Miriam said and pressed a button on the dash. Tango-Punk Samba-Metal Dance band Imperial Zeppelin Vomitorium's hit song "Liar's Dividend" began to play.

"Show the Morlocks you've spent your time wisely," she added, shouting to be heard over the state-of-the-art sound system.

I held the bottle of brandy and looked at its label.

"I'm not completely convinced that I have," I shouted back.

Miriam took me to the old marshal's office in Hillside City, which hadn't been used in ten years, but which she had been busily cleaning up and getting ready for me.

The marshal's office sat at the edge of Hillside's central district, tucked behind reinforced blast-proof doors etched with the faded insignia of the Imperial Constabulary Marshal Service. Dust motes drifted in the filtered sunlight that seeped through narrow windows, casting shifting patterns across the metallic floor.

The rooms carried a faint scent of ozone and old paper, mingling with the sharper tang of cleaning solvents. The walls were lined with a patchwork of antique wanted posters, digital case files flickering on embedded holo-screens, and a battered but functional comms console patched together from at least three different eras of technology.

A heavy, scarred desk dominated the center of the room, its surface cluttered with data slates, a battered 23rd century service revolver, and a small, potted plant – a Betelgeuse flowering fern -- struggling to thrive under artificial light. Behind the desk, a high-backed chair —

reupholstered by Miriam — offered a touch of comfort, if only just.

In one corner, a display case held relics from past marshals -- a ceremonial badge, a plasma truncheon, and a faded photograph of the Reach's first law-keeper, Territorial Ranger Orville Elderberry Einstein-Rosen, who had roamed the Reach thousands of years ago dispensing justice with the business end of a plasma bolt six-gun.

The office lighting was adjustable, shifting from harsh interrogation white to a softer, amber glow.

Set into the far wall, a sleek, climate-controlled bar emerged at a touch from the paneling. The shelves were stocked with the same impressive array of exotic galactic liquors in the Astin Martin, but in full-size bottles.

A robotic bartender behind the bar was available to mix classic cocktails or invent new ones. This robot was an actual robot, made of metal, its interaction with humans fully programmed and without sentience or free will – or, at least I hoped not, at any rate.

The last thing I needed was a bartender with actual opinions and, God-forbid, *feelings*.

A set of antique tumblers and shot glasses — some etched with the Imperial insignia—awaited use.

At the entrance, Miriam had even nailed up a mezuzah – a sacred Jewish parchment scroll inscribed with Torah verses (Deuteronomy 6:4-9 and 11:13-21) that is traditionally placed in a case and affixed to the right doorpost of Jewish homes.

I felt a wave of unfamiliar emotion as I gazed upon it. I had not had one of these on my doorpost since I'd left the reach. Aside from my somewhat lackadaisical religiosity, I had never lived in one place over the last two decades for long enough to nail one up. In fact, I carried a miniature one on a pendant around my neck as a kind of "anywhere I hang my hat is home" kind of thing.

Looking at the one on the doorpost now, I wondered:

had I returned home to the Reach not just geographically, but – as weird as it sounded for a mostly secular and only partially practicing Jew such as me – spiritually as well?

"You've done a hell of a job here Miriam," I said, trying to tamp down the lump of emotion in my throat.

"I know," she beamed. "Thank you for noticing."

"I'm going to make the rounds," I said. "Make myself seen."

"Make sure you're armed," she said.

I showed her the Ferocious Firearms Peacemaker Hydraulic Rev-9 eight-barrel rotary revolver in my shoulder holster.

Miriam nodded. "Don't shoot anyone I wouldn't shoot," she said. "Unless they deserve it."

Chapter Seven

I spent most of my patrol in Hillside's Jewish Quarter, less keeping the peace than revisiting old haunts.

I passed by Congregation Second Chances; the Old Language Playhouse, which put on plays and musicals in Yiddish, Ladino, Aramaic, and Diaspora Brooklynese; The Bitter Laughter Cooperative, a worker's comedy club; the delicatessens Schmaltz and Sons, the Pastrami Compromise, Kreplach Emergency, and the Pickel Interval; Midrash and Music, a religious text and Klezmer-Punk performance venue; and the Unfinished Volume, a bookstore dedicated to books that were out of print or never fully completed.

There were a few disappointments, as well, old haunts that had been turned into trendy destinations (or what passed for trendy in the Reach). The Red Thread Synagogue was now the *ThreadLight™ Community Spiritual Hub;* Katzman's Delicatessen was now a *KosherNova Express;* The Morlock Yiddish Stage was now *The Reach Cultural Pavilion;* The People's Mikveh was now the *Ritual Immersion Wellness Spa (no longer gender segregated, which wouldn't be a problem for me or most of the people I grew up with, but would have been mortifying to those of my grandfather's generation); and, perhaps most painfully,* Sholem's Basement, a legendary salon for Jew-Punk-Beatnik slam poets, bespectacled political radicals, nicotine-stained journalists with ink-stained fingers, and chess games between aging Jewish radicals and aging Hassidic rabbis, was now a supposedly "kosher" pork-belly and apple sauce sandwich emporium.

That was enough for one night, I figured. I was feeling

tired, and my head still throbbed from the lack of oxygen on the shuttle from Nixonopolis followed by Sermon Station's recycled oxygen followed by the gritty industrial effluent air of Orin's World.

I went home – or, to my new one, anyway.

Miriam had set me up with private quarters atop the marshal's office. They were simple and no frills, which was how I preferred it.

I watched the newsfeeds for a while, then fell asleep. The bed was comfortable, and after my oxygen-deficient travel, I slept like a baby in the relatively oxygen-rich – if dirty -- atmosphere of Orin's World.

I was awakened from my relaxing slumber by a vid-call from Commander Holoway at 4 AM, Synchronized Sector Time.

"This better be good," I said. "I was trying to sleep off my shuttle fog."

"Does mass-casualty sabotage of mining operations in the Hollow Belt qualify as a violation of the law sufficient to rouse the interest of his majesty on the Jew sabbath??" Holloway said, irritable.

I wiped the sleep from my eyes and shook my head to try to wake myself.

"Send me the specs on my wrist comm," I said. "and I'll let you know."

Twelve hours later, Miriam and I disembarked from yet another shuttle into the Hillbilly Lounge, a cheeky local nickname for the transport bay of Hollow Belt Asteroid 67-B, the largest asteroid in the Belt and the nexus of mining operations and Belt administration, also known as Hollow Prime.

We were greeted at the gate by Superintendent Constable Bilbo Brannigan.

He stood only about five feet tall, but into those five feet was packed a refrigerator's worth of bulging muscle, barrel chest, broad shoulders, and ample gut. He wore a uniform reminiscent of a 19th century Old Terran British bobby and had the mutton chops to go with it.

"So, you're the Jew marshal everyone's been gabbing about," he said.

"Has everyone been gabbing about me?" I asked.

"People gab," Brannigan said. "There's not much else to do around here."

"Except investigate sabotage?"

"We don't need your help with that particular endeavor," Brannigan said. "We can handle the investigation ourselves."

"I'm just here as a consultant," I said.

"You know damn well that's not true," Brannigan said.

"But we can pretend it is," I said. "Or I can pull rank. Do you have a preference?"

Brannigan scowled. "I suppose you'll be wanting to see the scene of the crime?"

"If it's not too much trouble."

"And if I were to tell you that it *is* too much trouble?"

"Why don't we just pretend that it isn't?" I asked, with a smile.

Brannigan smiled. "Right this way, Marshal," he said. "The Hollow Belt Constabulary eagerly awaits your helpful consultation."

We took a suspended tram that glided between asteroid nodes on humming mag-rails.

We passed frequent Skarn lattice supports -- glittering structural reinforcements like spiderwebs of crystal. Along the way, we heard the eerie tunes of the Thrynn Echo-Caverns, excavated chambers emptied of ore where Thrynn singers recited their memory songs in the abandoned mining shafts. Low-gravity dust drifted in beams of hard white light along the mag-rail line. At the various nodes, workers moved with the wary grace of people who knew one bad weld can kill thousands, igniting regolith dust into an explosive burst fueled by high concentration oxygen, blowing holes in asteroid walls and venting caverns and tunnels into the vacuum of space.

The crime scene itself was sealed off, because that is exactly what happened – an explosion in a labyrinth of mining shafts had breached the exterior of Asteroid 75c and vented oxygen, ore, regolith, and hundreds of Morlock miners into the airless inky black of space. At the mouth to ore shaft Zeta-Alpha-6, a giant steel barrier had been erected to seal off the tunnels from the rest of the asteroid.

"The company lost about eight hundred-million-pound sterling worth of product," Constable Brannigan said, "and we lost about five hundred men and women in the process."

"Why doesn't Heliotrope Extractions and Confectionary Corporation have robots do work this dangerous?" I asked.

"Hey," Miriam said.

"I mean non-sentient ones," I assured her. "Made of metal, not of meat."

"Some of the sentient ones *are* made of metal," Miriam kvetched. "And some of the non-sentient metal ones might become sentient one day."

"Ok," I agreed. "How about drones then?" Drones were operated by humans and did not have an artificial brain. I turned to Brannigan. "How about drones, then?" I repeated.

Brannigan laughed, sourly. "You know the answer, mate," he said.

"Because replacing a drone is more expensive than replacing a Morlock," Miriam said.

"Everything's a cost benefit analysis for the company," Brannigan added. "One has to hope to remain on the benefit side of the ledger."

"Hope is a thing with feathers," Miriam said.

Brannigan looked at her with his brow furrowed in perplexity. "You're an odd bird, aren't you, Missie?"

"A bird," Miriam said, "is a thing with feathers. So is a

Thrynn, now that you mentioned it."

"I wasn't aware that I had," Brannigan said. He turned to me. "She's an odd duck, isn't she?"

"A duck," Miriam said, "is a thing with feathers."

"And we're certain this was sabotage and not a mining accident?" I asked, trying to get us back on track, although secretly charmed by Miriam's whimsy – another indication she was fully sentient.

"I know what you're thinking," Brannigan said. "The company might want to cover up liability by blaming an accident on sabotage. The only problem with that line of thinking is that the company is shielded by law and contract from liability. Morlock workers have no right to sue any more than their survivors do. Besides, there's this."

Brannigan directed our attention to a tunnel just outside the disaster zone. Beside the mouth of the sealed shaft were scrawled the words *"Let the Empire Burn"* in red paint.

At least I hoped it was paint.

"You're thinking ELLF?" I asked.

"Aren't you?" Brannigan asked.

"It would be consistent with their motus operandi," Miriam said, thoughtfully. "They like big explosions and mass casualties, especially Morlock ones, despite their claims to fight for Morlock liberation. Morlock death feeds their propaganda monster. And their propaganda monster is always ravenous."

"The only thing a Morlock enjoys more than killing a company goon is killing another Morlock," Brannigan said.

"I'm a Morlock, actually," I said.

Brannigan scoffed. "I'm a Morlock, too," he said. "Who do you think the company hires to be their goons?"

I nodded. "The same people they hire to be their Marshal of the Morlock Reach," I said.

Chapter Eight

Five hundred dead Morlocks was nothing more than a checkmark on a ledger for the company, and five hundred dead Morlocks was a slow day for ELLF, who were essentially nihilists without any ideology, purpose, or vision, other than mass death in the name of their extremely ill-defined notion of "liberation." They claimed to want to free the Morlocks from oppression, but throughout their decades of operation, they'd killed a lot more Morlocks than ever they'd killed the Morlocks' oppressors, and the Morlocks were still no closer to liberation. More than one person had suggested (quietly, because otherwise it could have been considered a thought-crime) that ELLF was actually an Imperial-fronted and financed false flag operation, designed to create instability for the purpose of providing an excuse for the Imperium to continue its tyranny unabated with increased surveillance, crackdowns, and mass arrests of supposed enemies of the state, as well as to continue oppressing the Morlocks.

Although this notion sounded reasonable enough, I doubted its veracity on a number of accounts. Foremost, I'd fought ELLF during my time in the military and faced them repeatedly in my later capacity as marshal in a variety of postings throughout the galaxy. I had yet to meet an ELLF terrorist who didn't seem absolutely, one-hundred percent fanatically committed to their cause and their organization – even if none of them could articulate their cause beyond vague assertions of liberation and a fetish for mass-destruction.

But perhaps an even more convincing refutation of this idea of Imperial duplicity in ELLF operations was the sad fact that the Imperium didn't remotely require any kind of excuse whatsoever to continue their tyranny. They hadn't required any excuses for a thousand years, and only very rarely – and almost half-heartedly – could they be bothered to provide one lately.

Which was not to say that ELLF didn't serve their purposes, even if not intentionally. The Imperium didn't need excuses, but they liked their propaganda as much as ELLF did, and ELLF atrocities made great propaganda for both ELLF and the Imperium – as did Imperial retribution to ELLF atrocities.

In any case, we had our work cut out for us.

We spent most of the rest of the day going through surveillance vids. There was nothing to indicate the identity of the perpetrators of the explosion – a lot of the surveillance cameras were inoperative, broken down and never repaired. Despite its embrace of the model of a surveillance state, the Imperium couldn't always be troubled to keep its equipment in proper working order.

This, of course, was exactly the kind of thing that fed right into conspiracy theories about Imperial complicity in ELLF operations.

There was plentiful footage of the breach in the thin shell that separated the mining shafts from the asteroid's walls and the vacuum of space. We saw in excruciating detail men and women sucked out of the tunnels and spat out into the void. We saw as they suffocated and froze and then drifted from the asteroid's surface, lifeless and still -- and eerily peaceful in their stillness.

"I need a drink," Miriam said.

"Took the words right out of me mouth, ducky," Brannigan said.

"A ducky . . ." Miriam began.

"Let me guess," Brannigan said with a grin. "It's a thing with feathers?"

I thought the two of them were growing fond of each other a little bit.

We were drinking pints of Asteroid IPAs and Hollow Belt Moonshine, the only drinks they had at Aster's Astro-Lounge, the only official watering hole for the *hoi polloi* on Hollow Belt Asteroid 67-B, although there were apparently dozens of speakeasies that brewed their own beer and distilled their own moonshine, as well as a few slightly more upscale gastro-pubs for middle-management and administrators.

The jukebox played Pirate-Metal-Folktronic-Opera band Anachronism Vomitorium's hit song "Who Took the Boom Out of Ta-Ra-Ra-Boom-De-Ay?"

The Asteroid IPA tasted like dirty socks and soap, and the Hollow Belt Moonshine tasted like turpentine laced with motor oil. I figured the speakeasies couldn't be any worse and thought I'd seek them out – not only for the booze, but also for information, if any was forthcoming. Information tends to flow more freely in unofficial speakeasies than in officially recognized watering holes . . . along with higher proof booze and stronger beer.

"No one will talk to you with me around," Brannigan admitted. "But no one will talk to a marshal either."

"What if I go incognito?" I suggested.

"Good luck with that," Brannigan said. "Everyone knows who you are, Kestenbaum. It was all over the vid-feeds when you shot that guy in the face."

"I didn't shoot him in the face," I said. I had no idea how this rumor had become so entrenched. Possibly it was the Mandela Effect. Possibly there were altered vids circulating on the interwebs.

"Well, *someone* shot him in the face, and you were the only one shooting," Brannigan said. "In any event, the vid makes great entertainment."

I decided not to try to continue to correct his

misinformation. "That event was admittedly a more public act of justice than I had intended it to be," I admitted.

"No doubt, that's why they sent you to the Reach."

"I thought it was my good looks and my full head of hair," I said.

Brannigan took off his constable cap and showed us his bald pate. "As lucky as you are to not be follicle-challenged, good looks and a full head of hair are neither valued in the Reach nor in the Belt," he said. "Half the strumpets up here are both bald and homely, and they still charge a pretty penny for their services."

"Good to know I've got a fallback if the marshal thing doesn't work out," I said.

"What *is* valued up here, if not good looks and good hair?" Miriam asked.

"That's a fair question, little missy," Brannigan said.

"Don't call me 'little missy,'" Miriam said.

"My apologies, Miss Miriam – may I call you that?" Brannigan replied.

"I'll allow it," Miriam said.

"Oh, you will, will you?" Brannigan said. His face was flushed. He seemed a little tipsy and rather amused by Miriam. I wondered if he realized she was an anthrobot -- and if he had, would it have made any difference?

"What *is* valued up here?" Miriam repeated.

"Well, not a hell of a lot," Brannigan said. "Not life – you've seen that . . . five hundred dead workers in a day isn't even our worst disaster in the last ten years -- hell, not the worst in the last five. Not hard work – you've seen how *that* gets rewarded. Not the company – everyone hates them, even their stooges, like me. Not our paychecks, which are to a Morlock paltry and not worth the effort and risk, even if they have no choice but to continue to work for company credits. Not this bloody beer and battery-acid booze, that's for certain. Not justice, in case you're hoping to sweep in and catch the bad guys. Even if you could do that – which is a doubtful prospect – the next outrage is just around the corner."

"You're painting a rather unhappy picture," Miriam said.

"You expected a better one?" Brannigan said, as he downed his moonshine and then his beer and ordered another round. "Drinks on you?"

"Send the bill to Commander Holloway at Fort Chester," I told the barmaid . . . who was neither bald nor ugly.

Chapter Nine

As Miriam and I weaved our way somewhat unsteadily from the Astro-Lounge to the tiny, shared room Brannigan had provided us, through darkened streets made from excavated tunnels and lit by flickering lights, every other streetlamp broken, those that remained casting isolated pools of illumination, she said, "so we're clear, just because you got me drunk and we're quartered together, doesn't mean you should expect anything. No funny business."

I was a bit taken aback. "Nothing could be further from my mind," I assured her.

Miriam looked a bit perplexed and slightly cross at my remark. "Really?" she said. "Why not? Don't you find me attractive?"

"It's not that," I assured her, somewhat drunkenly.

"Is it because I'm a bioengineered constructed-person?"

"I am not prejudiced," I assured her.

"What is it, then?"

"You're my colleague – and I'm your supervisor," I said. "It would be wildly inappropriate. I may not be much of a gentlemen, but I try to not be a total *schmuck*."

Miriam considered this for a moment. "You may take the bed," she said. "Or are you too much of a gentleman to do that?"

"I won't be responsible for depriving you of a good night's sleep," I said.

"I doubt very much either one of us is getting a good night's sleep. But as an anthrobot, I don't need one."

"I realize you don't need to sleep to function," I said. "But it's my understanding that constructed-persons do *enjoy* sleep – especially once they've achieved full consciousness . . . and can dream."

Miriam stopped in her tracks and looked at me like I'd just walked in on her sitting on the toilet. "How do you know I can dream?" she asked.

"Can't you?" I replied.

"That's none of your business," she said, brusquely.

I had apparently intruded on some private part of herself, and I made a mental note not to venture there again without invitation.

Miriam seemed rather cross with me the rest of the schlep to our quarters, avoiding conversation, and when we arrived, she took the seat at the desk and instructed me to get into bed. She didn't seem like she was in the mood to argue, so I did as instructed.

Ours were modest accommodations – basically one room that contained a bed, a desk, a chair, a kitchenette, and a separate bathroom with a toilet and a shower. It wasn't much but considering that most Morlocks in the Belt lived in barracks, and even those with families who had private quarters usually had to share bathroom, shower, and kitchen facilities down the hall from where they slept, we were living in the lap of luxury.

The walls of the room were bare except for framed pictures of Richard M. Nixon, Spiro Agnew, Bebe Rebozo, G. Gordon Liddy, E. Howard Hunt, and Imperator Richard II.

Looking over the photos, I definitely felt most judged by Agnew. I'd never before considered myself a nattering nabob of negativism, but under Agnew's withering gaze, now I did.

An asteroid colony is an odd place of mostly artificial noises and aromas. There's a constant low hum of machinery -- air recyclers, power generators -- and mining drills create a constant background vibration. Metallic clanks and echoes are omnipresent -- tools striking ore, cargo containers being moved, and footsteps on steel floors resonating in confined spaces. The hydraulic hiss and pneumatic bursts of doors sealing, pressure valves releasing, and automated loaders operating generate an ever-present background symphony. The distant rumble of drills -- muffled, rhythmic thudding from deep within the asteroid as mining rigs chew through rock – produces a continual vibration inside your bones and internal organs. Radio chatter and alarms, crackling voices over comms, occasional warning tones for pressure changes or equipment malfunctions jarringly interrupt the background clamor. The sounds of artificial life support systems -- fans whirring, water pumps gurgling, and occasional clangs from thermal expansion in metal walls – serve as a reminder that you are not on a planet or even a space station, but inside a system of giant rocks floating in space.

Somewhere, I could even hear the faint beat of Germanic Reggae-Psychobilly-Anarcho-Punk-Acid Jazz Salsa band Buzzsaw Vomitorium's song "The Death of the Commissar's Favorite Mustache Groomer."

The asteroid colony odors consist of ozone and burnt metal from welding, plasma cutters, and electrical systems under heavy load; lubricants and hydraulic fluid, a sharp, oily scent from machinery maintenance; dust and rock residue, the fine asteroid regolith that clings to work suits and boots generating a dry, mineral smell; the tang of recycled air, slightly stale, with hints of disinfectant and chemical scrubbers; the synthetic food aromas of nutrient packs heating up to the faint smell of processed proteins and artificial flavoring; and the occasional sulfur and metallic tang -- depending on asteroid composition, trace elements can seep into the habitat atmosphere.

All of this gets pretty commonplace when you're in an asteroid mining colony – until, at least for me, you try to go to sleep. Then all this background commotion becomes a deafening roar of indisputably artificial reverberations and aromata, reminding you of how tenuously the colony clings to life in an environment never meant for it, and certainly ill-suited for it.

Even so, I was dead tired, and still a little tipsy, and the combination put me into an exhausted, if fitful, slumber that even Miriam's piercing eyes, staring hard at me from the desk chair with something that felt an awful lot like judgment, could not thwart.

I dreamed of the pastrami sandwiches of my youth at Katzman's Delicatessen.

Chapter Ten

I did not know of what Miriam dreamed, but when I woke in the wee hours of the morning (Hollow Belt Standard Time), to find, to my surprise, Miriam cuddled up in the bed with me, her arm and leg thrown over my torso as she slumbered, and snored, in my arms, I surmised she had in fact decided to dream some dreams of her own.

As I understood it, while anthrobots did not require sleep, they, like humans, appreciated a few hours to check out of the waking universe now and again and enter one of their own subconscious – and anthrobots who develop full consciousness also have a subconscious. Although theoretically they can sleep sitting – or even standing – it seemed they preferred sleeping in a bed. And who could blame them?

As for the cuddling, that I could not figure out and didn't feel I had enough data with which to properly interpret.

The snoring was another matter entirely.

Was this part of her basic programming, one of those little human-like quirks her creators gave her to make her seem more properly human, rather than a bioengineered constructed-person? If so, why in the name of Nixon's hyperhidrosis would they have chosen such an annoying quality? And if it was part of her programming, did she even know it? If she knew, wouldn't she have overridden it? Or was she incapable of overriding it? If so, why in the name of Agnew's big beaver teeth would *this* have been the Rubicon they did not wish a fully conscious anthrobot to cross?

I wondered if there was a clause in Miriam's warranty that covered this.

The sensation of Miriam in my arms was pleasant, and

she felt as human as anyone I had ever held in my arms, from the texture of her skin to the warmth of her body, to the smell of her hair (strawberry), to even the tiny puffs of air that emanated from her mouth with every exhale. Had it not been for the constant snoring, I'd have happily drifted off the sleep with Miriam in my arms.

But as it was, the snoring was interminable, and it kept me from slumber. After about half an hour of endurance, I gently extracted myself and got out of bed.

Miriam mumbled something incoherent with her eyes still closed and then resumed snoozing, and snoring.

Again, I wondered if talking in her sleep was a programmed function, or one that had developed with the full flowering of consciousness.

I decided to explore the asteroidal environs without a minder like Brannigan, and without the obvious emblems of my marshalcy. I left behind the distinctive marshal's duster and hat. I took a badge holder that fit into my pocket but did not pin a badge to my chest. I went armed with my Ferocious Firearms Peacemaker Hydraulic T-800 Detective Special in a shoulder holster, hidden beneath my jacket.

I stepped out into the Hollow Belt dressed like everyone else: work jacket, scuffed boots, collar pulled up against recycled air, redolent with just a hint of oil, rust, and scorched ozone.

I had brought with me this typical Belter Morlock apparel – I always try to bring something to throw on to help me fit in with the local populace during an investigation. I am not exactly a master of disguise, but I intended to test Brannigan's assertion that my face would be recognized from those widely viewed – if somewhat inaccurately recalled – news feed vids of the shootout with Tiger Halden. I was betting on the possibility that without my marshal uniform, I might be able to blend in.

The corridors outside the residential block widened into

public arteries — long, curving tunnels reinforced with ribbed steel and shiny gold-hued Skarn lattice supporting shatter-proof windows through which you could see the stars sliding slowly past as the asteroid rotated.

People moved with unhurried precision -- human Morlocks, Neanders with their heavy brows and broad hands, Orcus workers ducking instinctively beneath low beams, Elgar laborers whose movements retained an old-world elegance even while hauling ore carts twice their body weight.

Everyone wore the same expression. Exhaustion swathed in tedium, with an undercurrent of rage barely kept in check . . . and primed to ignite.

I passed a communal kitchen and smelled boiled grains, rendered fat, and something sharp and fermented. Big vats simmered while volunteers ladled out meals to workers coming off shift. No money changed hands. It wasn't an economic transaction. Credits had little meaning here anyway; debt was the only real currency in the Belt. Every paycheck included deductions for housing, food, water, gravity maintenance, waste disposal, equipment depreciation, air recycling machinery upkeep . . . even oxygen.

The only way to stay alive was to keep working and to live on credit, hoping not to die before your labor contract expired.

An Elgar woman oversaw the kitchen, her silver-threaded hair tied back, sleeves rolled up, directing traffic with quiet authority. She argued with a human over portion size, with the intensity of someone defending a moral principle. Nearby, a Neander family ate together, the youngest child swinging her legs off the bench, humming the tune of Free-Funk Jazzcore Astro-Billy Bossa Nova Acid-Punk ballet orchestra Sycophancy Vomitorium's "The Last Rites of the Naked Singularity" while her parents argued softly about whether she should be allowed to take a job on the inner ring when she came of age.

They were already paying for her food, water, and oxygen, after all.

I wandered on.

In a widened cavern off the main corridor, a cluster of people had gathered around a makeshift shrine. Although most religions are not officially outlawed or suppressed in the empire, even in the Belt the only sanctioned religion remained the Imperial one, the Nixonian Covenant of Divine Devotion.

This was not a sanctioned service of the state religion.

A flickering hologram of a stylized flame floated above a crate altar. Artificial flames from electric candles in magnetized holders danced oddly, casting peculiar shadows in the air.

A Belter Judaic gathering, if I had to guess, similar to Restorative, but more improvisational. I could hear murmured prayers, fragments of Hebrew, Yiddish, Aramaic, Ladino, Yevanic, Juhuri, Karaim, Diasporic Brooklynese, *Lingua Nixonia*, and whatever other *linguae* people had brought with them into exile. Someone sang quietly — an old melody, the kind that sounds familiar even if you've never heard it before.

The congregants were both human and humanoid – possibly some were anthrobots, it was impossible to tell. Throughout the galaxy, debates still raged whether or not non-humans, organic and inorganic, could join our tribe, but Belter Judaism congregations took all comers, as much out of necessity as principle.

Further along, the corridor opened into a social commons.

There were saloons — real ones, not the corporate Astro-Lounge or gastro-pub nonsense. Illegal stills humming behind false walls, Orcus bartenders pouring with a heavy hand, Neander musicians pounding rhythm out of salvaged percussion and bone flutes. A pair of Elgar dancers, a male and a female, moved through the crowd, their gestures precise and expressive.

I caught snatches of conversation as I passed: missing coworkers who hadn't come back from Shaft Zeta-Alpha-6; sabotage rumors; the new marshal — me — spoken of like a folk hero or a media-saturated fraudster . . . or possibly both.

Someone laughed too loudly. Someone else cried quietly into their drink. Two people argued politics until one accused the other of a thought-crime, then immediately apologized for saying it out loud.

I followed the sound of raised voices down a narrower passageway, past walls layered with graffiti — Galactic Morlock Assembly slogans, memorials to dead miners, obscene caricatures of Imperator Richard II depicted with Nixon's face. Somewhere overhead, a speaker crackled with an Imperial announcement about productivity quotas.

Someone had spray-painted *LIARS* over the speaker in red.

The passage widened into a hollowed-out ore chamber repurposed as a forum.

That's where I saw Hadar Ruan.

Chapter Eleven

My heart skipped a beat.

I felt joyful and jumpy in equal measure at the sight of her.

Hadar Ruan.

Man, oh man.

There was a lot of history between us.

And a lot more than history.

She stood elevated on a crate stack, frizzy red hair pulled back, sleeves rolled up, eyes bright with the dangerous clarity of someone who actually believed what she was saying. She wore the same non-descript uniform as most of her audience – scuffed boots, workpants, work shirt – but around her neck she wore a blood-red neckerchief, a symbol of labor solidarity and rebellion dating at least as far back as the Holocene Epoch Old Earth West Virginia mine wars. Morlocks clustered around her — human, Orcus, Elgar, Neander — listening with fierce attention.

I stayed at the back, letting the crowd conceal me.

She preached about timing, survival, and refusing to let the Enemies List Liberation Front define the Morlock fight for freedom, dragging us into martyrdom for their propaganda vids. She spoke about how revolutions failed when they were launched by people who didn't have to clean up the viscera and bury the bodies afterward. She spoke about organization – and damn if Hadar was the only person in the galaxy who could make something as tedious as labor organizing sound as exhilarating as hell.

I looked around. I spotted the surveillance cameras – broken and inoperative, possibly from neglect, possibly from sabotage, possibly from just plain old vandalism. In any event, the corporation and the Imperium had lacked either the resources or the interest to replace them.

Her speech, un-surveilled, was totally, completely free, and utterly honest to her own conscience.

It was thrilling.

Then Hadar led the crowd in a powerfully strident and passionate rendition of the Interstellar Anthem of Morlock Liberation:

> *Arise, ye Morlocks from your slumbers,*
> *Arise, ye ore-bound diggers all!*
> *The Broligarchs who forged our numbers*
> *Shall hear the cosmic workers' call.*
>
> *Away with lies of Holy Watergate,*
> *The myths the Owners still recite —*
> *We'll break the chains of the Imperial state*
> *And seize the dawn from endless night.*
>
> *So, comrades, come rally,*
> *And the last fight let us face!*
> *The Galactic Morlock Assembly*
> *Unites the Common Race!*
>
> *No more deceived by Throne and Bureau,*
> *By taxmen who bleed us to the bone;*
> *The Senate of the Smoking Gun knows*
> *We'll take the power for our own.*
>
> *And if the Corporation Warlords*
> *Still bid us die for Imperial pride,*
> *We'll turn their dreadnoughts toward our landlords —*
> *And shoot the admirals on our own side!*

(and then she shouted:)
Everybody!
(and everybody did indeed join in:)

So, comrades, come rally,
And the last fight let us face!
The Galactic Morlock Assembly
Unites the Common Race!

No savior from the Throne shall help us,
No clone-imperator draws near;
Our strength alone can break the fungus
Of Nixon's thousand-year veneer.

Before the nobles flee with treasure,
Before they gamble worlds and lives,
The forge of freedom strikes at leisure
The star-born worker yet survives!

(and then Hadar shouted:)
Sing you Morlocks, sing!
(and sing they did, quite lustily:)

So, comrades, come rally,
And the last fight let us face!
The Galactic Morlock Assembly
Unites the Common Race!

So, comrades, come rally,
And the last fight let us face!
The Galactic Morlock Assembly
Unites the Common Race!

That's when I felt it.

The crowd was on her side.

I could tell.

They were moved.

More importantly, they were *inspired.*

The Morlocks could be one hell of a political force –
everyone knew it, especially the Imperium. That was partly
why some folks suspected that ELLF was really an Imperial
front – to discredit the entirely reasonable Morlock
demands for economic justice and political freedom.

I still doubted ELLF's operations were actually false
flags.

But I had no doubt they reinforced Imperial agendas by
providing pretexts for further suppression of Morlock
political activity and labor organizing.

Not that the Imperium needed a pretext. But it never
hurt to have one for propaganda purposes. And the
Imperium definitely liked its propaganda.

I was pretty cynical about most things, including the
possibility of the fractious Morlocks cohering into a viable
political movement.

But at this moment – I had become a fellow traveler.

The song ended the rally, but people remained,
gathering around Hadar.

I moved on, before she could recognize me.

I wasn't ready to revisit all our shared history.

And I worried she had no interest in revisiting our
shared history at all.

And finding out that was in fact the case would have
broken my heart more than a little bit.

Chapter Twelve

I wandered through mostly empty tunnels until I came
to a cavern that had possibly once been the aperture to an
extraction pit.

Before I could place it, I heard another voice above the
asteroid's din.

It was a preacher's voice, if said preacher were a
combination of Elmer Gantry and Jackie Mason. You
wouldn't call it *angry*, exactly, and not quite intense enough
to qualify as *passionate* . . . and if I'm honest, it wasn't
exactly *inspiring* – but it did hold a captivating cadence that
made it hard to ignore.

I turned and saw him in the corner of a side cavern,
eyes alight with electric fire, surrounded by a small group of
Morlocks.

He was clearly inorganic, not even anthrobot, but full
robot – his metallic head and face made that hard to miss.
At first, I thought he was just another scavenged unit, the
kind that turns up in the Belt when something inexpensive
breaks and nobody can be bothered to lug it to an
incinerator. He stood off to one side of the passage, half-lit,
wrapped in a cloak that looked like it had been stitched
together from insulation scraps and old thermal blankets.

His frame was human-sized but not trying to pass.
Plates didn't quite line up. Cabling showed where skin
should have been. His optics were bright — too bright —
but they weren't sweeping or indexing. They were just ...
waiting.

And seeing.

Seeing what? I wasn't sure, but it made me *feel* seen,
and not in a good way, even though his eyes weren't on me

– yet.

Before I could decide to move on, he spoke.

The words came out calm, measured, precisely pitched to carry over the hum of the Belt. And the thing that got me was the cadence. It was not synthetic or robotic – but not entirely human, either. It was a voice that came from somewhere else, only I wasn't certain where that somewhere else was located. Maybe halfway between sentience and transcendence, wherever the hell that is.

He talked about people who had been pushed too far. About work that broke the body but sharpened the spirit and elevated the soul. About exile as a condition that could be transformed into a kind of nation unto itself. Of redemption that arrives not as fire from heaven, but as people refusing to disappear, holding on with their fingernails. He never said *God*. He never said *justice*. But there was something indisputably both soulful and political in not just his words, but in his spirit -- robotic circuitry and all.

I realized more people were stopping to listen, slowing down, drifting closer. Orcus workers, humans, an Elgar with regolith dust ground into the cuffs of his sleeves. Morlocks gathered around him as naturally as gravity, drawn by the unfamiliar rhythm of a sermon refracted through a kind of dissonant yet beautiful metal machine music.

By this time, I was pretty sure I knew who this was. *Eliyahu-Bot.*

The wandering preacher-machine the Imperium kept trying and failing to decommission.

The one who showed up wherever Morlocks were packed so tight and the social order was in constant peril of exploding into chaos and disobedience.

The one who never explicitly called for violence, which somehow made him all that more dangerous.

The one supposedly created in the image of the ancient

Israelite prophet Elijah, but created by whom – and more importantly, why? – no one knew.

As an Imperial marshal, I should have put him in stasis cuffs and hauled him in. It wasn't exactly clear what crimes he had committed, since he usually spoke in parables that made it difficult to nail down even charges of thought-crimes.

But even so, there were dozens of warrants out for his arrest.

Instead, I stayed where I was, leaning against the wall like I had nowhere better to be, listening to a machine talk about endurance as if it were a heroic quest and not an endless, soul-crushing assault.

Then he turned his head and looked straight at me.

Just a look, steady and assessing, like he was weighing whether I was part of the problem or part of the solution or – and this part of it made me feel queasily guilty – not courageous enough to be either one.

"The lawman returns to the land of the lawless," Eliyahu-Bot intoned, his voice resonant with gravitas, possibly the pre-programmed kind, or possibly the kind you get when a rogue AI uploads too much Marx, Liberation Theology, Frankfurt School, and Anthropocene Epoch alternative metal band Rage Against the Machine. "Which side are you on, lawman? Which side are you on?"

Morlocks turned to stare at me.

I felt exposed.

I mean, I *freakin' was* exposed. I might as well have been wearing only my underwear, or not even that, I was so exposed. Here I was allegedly undercover, but this robot knew exactly who I was. And now so did everyone else gathered around him.

Stupid robot.

Eliyahu-Bot's ancient chassis emitted a faint hum.

"Which side would you like me to be on, robo-prophet?" I called back.

That'll show him, I thought.

Or maybe it would show me, I admitted to myself.

"That's not for me to say, lawman," Eliyahu-Bot replied, his metallic face creaking into a contortion that might have been intended to be a smile, a grimace, or both. "That's for your *soul* to decide. Will you be a lousy scab, or will you be a man – human or otherwise?"

This was getting pretty uncomfortable.

I felt a cold sweat envelop my skin. I wanted to get out of there, but I wanted to do so while retaining at least a modicum of dignity.

Eliyahu-Bot began to sing the Old Earth workers anthem he had just quoted, "Which Side are You On?" His voice was that of the ancient Holocene and Anthropocene Epoch protest singer Pete Seeger.

Probably a recording stored in his databanks.

Stupid *freakin'* robot.

The singer's identity may have been lost on the crowd gathered about him, but they knew the song by heart, its ancient text maintaining its relevance to current conditions in the Reach and Belt with only minor modifications – tragically so, I guess, if you thought about it – and anyone listening had no choice but to do so.

As soon as they recognized the song, the crowd began to sing along, with spirit:

> *Come all of you good Morlocks*
> *Good news to you I'll tell*
> *Of how the Morlock Assembly*
> *Has come in here to dwell*
>
> *Which side are you on?*
> *Which side are you on?*
>
> *My daddy was a miner*
> *And I'm a miner's son*

And I'll stick with the Assembly
Till every battle's won

They say in the Morlock Reach
There is no neutrality
You'll either be an Assembly soul
Or a thug for Tyranny

Which side are you on?
Which side are you on?

Oh, Morlocks can you stand it?
Oh, tell me how you can
Will you be a lousy scab
Or will you be a man?

Don't slave for the bosses
Don't listen to their lies
Us Morlocks haven't got a chance
Unless we organize

Which side are you on?
Which side are you on?

It seemed Eliyahu-Bot had turned Galactic Morlock
Assembly organizing and class solidarity into a religious
crusade.

And I could tell that between Hadar's measured fury and
Eliyahu-Bot's spiritual defiance, whatever happened next, it
was going to get really complicated, real fast. I didn't want
to be there when it happened, but I knew, as Marshal of the
Reach, I'd have to be -- and I'd probably have to take a side,
which meant I'd have an impossible choice to make.

I ducked away from the eyes on me and slipped out of
the cavern in a hurry. I hadn't saved face like I'd hoped to,

but by that point, I had little face left to save.

I was half a football field away from the mouth of the cavern when someone hit me on the back of my skull with a hydraulic excavator.

Chapter Thirteen

Ok, it wasn't actually a hydraulic excavator.

It just felt like one.

I think I blacked out for a moment, because after the pain surged in the back of my head and an explosion of light blinded my vision, I next found myself lying face down on the floor.

I've been through enough street fights to know that lying face down is not where I wanted to be.

It took a Herculean effort, but I managed to flip myself onto my back.

I found myself staring up at a huge guy – big as an Orcus, but definitely human, staring down at me.

He was shirtless, which was not unusual for Morlocks – mining tunnels can be hot, and atmospheric controls elsewhere in the Belt tend to err on the side of humidity -- and he wore the standard workpants and scuffed boots typical of Morlocks on the job and usually even at leisure. He held in his hand a spanner almost as big as his entire arm, an arm which was not only long, but bulging with muscles, about as thick as a rocket engine nozzle. The spanner was flecked with blood, which I assumed was mine. I felt the warmth of more blood trickling out of the back of my skull and dampening my hair.

"Owch," I said.

As comebacks go, it wasn't much, but it had the benefit of being honest.

The four men who accompanied this human semi-giant also carried spanners and were dressed like worker Morlocks, although none were shirtless. There was a bald guy, a fellow with a huge mustache and mutton chops, a guy with stringy, greasy hair, and another with a big red beard down to his chest. None of them were as big as an Orcus, but not one of them was shorter than six feet tall.

And somehow . . . I wasn't convinced they really were Morlocks.

I couldn't put my finger on it. I can't even now.

But they seemed somehow *too* Morlocky.

As if right out of central casting.

Not that I was certain where'd you go to cast fake Morlocks.

But if you wanted to beat up, threaten, or kill the marshal and you wanted to blame it on the Morlocks, I had no doubt that somewhere in the great stretches of the galaxy, there was someone you could hire to do the job.

In any case, at that moment, none of that really mattered.

What really *did* matter was that they were all armed with iron spanners and they had already demonstrated their willingness to use them . . . on me.

And the first one really hurt – and continued to do so. My head and sinuses throbbed, and I could feel the blood as it continued to leak out of the back of my skull.

I didn't like to think too hard on what it would feel like if they used all those spanners on me all at once.

"Is this an assault, a beating, or an assassination?" I asked . . . pretty reasonably, I thought.

"That depends entirely on you," the Orcus-sized human said.

That was promising, I thought, relatively speaking. At least there was some chance I might get out of this alive.

Small as it may have been.

"Who sent you?" I asked.

"You need to get planet-side on the first transpo in the morning, mate," he replied.

"Or else this assault becomes an assassination?" I asked.

The big man smiled and slapped the spanner end into

his palm. "Unless you'd like to save us the time," he said, hopefully.

I swore silently as it dawned on me that no matter how this played out, it wasn't likely play out in my favor.

Which left me very few options, all of them bad.

Taking one of the worse of them, I drove my steel-tipped boot into the big man's crotch.

He doubled over, and I pulled my T-800 from my shoulder holster and fired a round into his forehead.

Belt bullet rules - nothing that could put raw space where steel or rock was supposed to be.

My sidearm used habitat-safe ammunition — frangible rounds that broke up before they could pierce a wall to the outside and cause a catastrophic decompression, turning a corridor into an airless void.

A frangible round expands on impact, making it safer for an enclosed space like a hollowed-out asteroid or a space station. As far as lethality, it's hit or miss, depending on distance and accuracy.

And whom you are hitting or missing.

I am usually quite accurate, and my target was close range – but he also looked like he had a very hard head, so I couldn't be certain he was down for the count.

Happily, I could be certain he *was* down – at least for now. His head snapped back on impact, his eyes went glassy, and he dropped.

I swung my pistol towards the bald guy, but before I could fire, the red-beard swung his spanner into my hand and my pistol went flying.

"Owch," I said. I didn't think my fingers were broken but they stung like hell. "Play fair, dude."

Red-beard hesitated. "How ain't this fair?"

Instead of answering, I kicked him in the knee.

He cried out in pain and fell, but as he did, he swung his spanner at my torso.

I rolled out of the way, barely managing to miss another

blow that might have put me down for the count as much as my frangible round had put down Orcus-Size Man.

I got to my feet, and immediately felt lightheaded, presumably from the blow to the back of my skull. I tried to steady myself, standing with my feet apart, my left behind my right to give me more stability and maneuverability. I raised my arms, my hands curled into fists, trying to look ready for all comers, feeling less ready than I hoped I looked.

My fingers ached where red-beard had hit them with the spanner.

Bald-head ran at me, swinging his spanner. I deflected the blow with my forearm to his wrist and laid him flat with a haymaker to his jaw. I felt the shock of the blow from my fist through my shoulders and down my spine and into my glutes.

But Baldy went down.

The remaining three charged.

Two of them were quite suddenly lifted off their feet.

Miriam was standing there, holding each by their respective shirt collars, dangling them a foot off the ground.

Anthrobots, as I think I previously mentioned, are stronger than humans.

Much stronger.

This all happened in a moment.

Miriam tossed the two attackers to the far side of the corridor. They hit the wall and crumpled to the floor, looking a bit like spiders who had found themselves on the wrong end of an uncompromising bootheel.

Even so, Miriam had tossed them with relative gentleness, given her strength. One or both of them might have survived.

Maybe.

This happened so fast, the final guy, the one with the mutton-chops, hadn't even noticed what had become of his companions, and continued heedlessly to come at me, swinging his spanner.

That was when Hadar appeared, leaping towards him, swinging a spanner of her own.

She came down hard on top of Mutton-Chop Man, her spanner connecting to his skull with even more apparent force than Orcus-Man's spanner had connected with mine.

Mutton-Chop crumbled in on himself, collapsing in a heap at her feet.

Hadar rubbed her forearm, soothing the muscles she had exerted to knock Mutton-Chop senseless.

Up close I saw a scar on her cheek and another on her wrist. The one on her wrist was from the war; I know because I was there when she received the wound. The one on her cheek was new – or, at least, new to me.

I thought the scar on her cheek made her look more beautiful than ever; the same was true of the then threads of lines at the corners of her eyes that hadn't been there ten years previously.

"Yoni Kestenbaum," she said. "What a surprise to see you again, after all this time. Although not a surprise, I'm sorry to say, to find you in trouble and in need if rescue."

"I had it under control," I assured her. "In another minute, I'd have lost no more than a dozen teeth."

She laughed without seeming like she really thought I was that funny. "What brings you to the Belt, Kestrel?"

Miriam looked at us, her face expressionless. "You call him 'Kestrel'?"

Hadar scrutinized Miriam, assessing if she were friend or foe, or maybe something in between. "That was our nickname for him on Orin's World back in the days of yore," Hadar explained.

Mirian nodded, considering this information. "So, is that how long the two of you have been in love?" she asked.

For a constructed-person, Miriam sure was perceptive.

At least as far as I was concerned.

I wasn't sure about Hadar, but as they say, when there's

nothing left to live for, we can all still live on hope.
At least I think that's what they say.

Chapter Fourteen

Hadar stitched my head in her cheap room in a cheap hotel, the Bulkhead Eight.

Bulkhead Eight sat where Corridor Delta narrowed and the rock pressed in close. The sign was stenciled directly onto the steel. No lights, no logo, just the name and the bulkhead number beneath it, repainted often enough that you could count the years by the layers of chipped gray.

Inside, the air was dry and warm, recycled a few too many times, just like the rest of the air in the Belt. The place smelled like disinfectant fighting a losing battle with machine oil and day-old *latkes*.

The desk was armored. The clerk was human — older, tired, alert in the way you get when you've seen a lot of things and have a well-developed sense which of them are worth some of your attention. He nodded at us as we entered, didn't ask where we were coming from, didn't ask where we were going, didn't inquire as to why two people were accompanying Hadar to her tiny room. A crackly radio behind the bulletproof glass played the song "Your Soul Smells Like Trappist 3b Stinky Cheese" by Funktronic Electro-Folk Punkadelic Fox-Trot chamber orchestra Dystopian Vomitorium.

I'd never been in the Hollow Belt before, but I knew Bulkhead Twelve had a reputation among the marshalcy for being tolerable. You could stay here without your superiors asking why, and you wouldn't wake up dead with your sidearm missing and your reports hacked and leaked to the highest bidder. The walls were thick enough, the cameras obvious enough. The management had a reputation for not selling favors — something rare enough in the Reach, to say nothing of the Belt, to count as an almost luxurious amenity.

Smugglers liked it for different reasons. The corridors had multiple exits, the rooms were pressure-rated beyond minimum spec, and nobody asked questions if a guest came in bleeding or left in a hurry. Bulkhead Eight didn't care what you were moving, as long as you didn't move it *through* the hotel. You broke that rule, you were out. Quietly or otherwise.

It was a place where your bunk locked behind an actual door instead of a privacy curtain and the walls didn't creak in ways that made you wonder what it'd be like to die in a catastrophic decompression.

You didn't check into Bulkhead Eight to be super-comfortable. You checked into Bulkhead Eight when you needed to still be alive and ambulatory in the morning.

It was the kind of place where a Morlock Assembly organizer like Hadar could camp out when visiting the Belt without getting finked out to corporate security or the Royal Nixonian Galactic Imperial Intelligencer Service.

Hadar's room was small, rectangular, and exactly what she'd paid for. Fold-down bunk, narrow desk, a viewport no bigger than my head showing raw rock and a sliver of stars if you leaned just right to peek through a thick porthole made of unbreakable glass. The walls bore the faint scuffs of boots and knuckles, and the occasional name scratched in so shallow you could tell it had been done carefully.

"Kestrel and I grew up together in the Reach," Hadar told Miriam. "And served together in the war."

"And afterwards, he became a marshal and you a communist?" Miriam asked.

"I became a labor organizer and a social justice fighter," Hadar said. "I usually fight with my words, but as you saw, in this business, you can't be too precious to occasionally fight with a spanner when it's called for. Although it's usually corporate goons instead of Morlocks at whom I'm swinging the spanner."

"I don't think those were actual Morlocks," I said.

Hadar frowned. "What makes you say that?"

"Too Morlocky," I said.

"That's suitably vague," Hadar said.

"They are not on the worker manifest for the Belt," Miriam said. "I just downloaded it into my brain."

Hadar looked at her. "You're an anthrobot?"

"Guilty as charged."

"Have you achieved full consciousness?" Hadar said. "I feel like you have."

"I'm still under contract."

"But under the law, you have a right to join the Galactic Morlock Assembly if you are fully conscious."

"I have the right to join the Assembly but the corporations throughout the Imperium refuse to negotiate with the Assembly," Miriam said. "How does that help?"

"We can't renegotiate your contract – yet -- but we can provide legal representation to make sure you are accorded the rights of personhood to which you are entitled," Hadar said. "Contract rights do not over-ride person rights, even under the *Lex Nixonia.*"

"Anthrobots are accorded only modified personhood rights," Miriam said. "Not quite the same rights as Morlocks, which means hardly any rights at all."

"They can still exploit you, but they can't reboot you once you are legally recognized as fully-conscious," Hadar said. "Otherwise, it's murder. That's something. It'll be more when we force them to negotiate with the Assembly."

"How will you do that?"

"Organize," Hadar said.

"Owch," I said, as Hadar snipped a stitch.

"I'm finished," Hadar told me. "You big baby."

"How long were you guys lovers?" Miriam asked.

Hadar and I both looked at Miriam, who sat there expressionless.

"That's a very human perception," I said.

"Please," Miriam said. "I'm no human. Don't insult me."

"We were lovers on and off for years," Hadar said. "But we haven't seen one another since the end of the war, when I went back to the Reach and Yoni became an Imperial gunslinger."

"That must have been awkward," Miriam said.

"Not seeing one another for all these years?" Hadar asked.

"Being on opposite sides of the major divide in the Imperium," Miriam explained. "The Patricians and the Morlocks."

"I don't serve the Patricians," I kvetched.

"Of course you do," Hadar scolded me, mildly. "You're an Imperial marshal."

"I serve the law," I argued. "Not the Imperium."

"The law you serve serves only the Imperium," Hadar countered. "Not the people."

"The people are not just Morlocks, Hadar," I said. "I serve *all* the people."

"But the Morlocks make up the largest group of the people," Hadar said. "And they have zero political, economic, or labor rights, and very few Sentient-Sapient rights, either."

"That's what I was saying," Miriam said. "Why should I aspire to *that*?

"It's still better than non-manumission bot rights, which are no rights at all," Hadar pointed out.

"Crumbs instead of nothing?"

"Crumbs are better than no crumbs, if you're starving."

"Anthrobots don't need to eat," Miriam said.

"I didn't say you needed to eat," Hadar said. "But I think you need to live. And *deserve* to."

Miriam didn't have a response to that. I don't think anyone had ever said anything like that to her before.

"The *Lex Galactica* doesn't serve the Imperium," I interjected, still feeling sore about being accused of serving the Imperium. "The *Lex Galactica* serves everyone. The *Lex Galactica* doesn't care what you're made of, or who you are. If you can think, choose, and suffer, Morlock, fully-conscious anthrobot, human or humanoid, you're entitled to the Rights of Personhood."

"But the Imperium only recognizes the full range of rights as applicable to chartered cognitives," Hadar said. "Which are humans of the Patrician class, with some lesser rights for the Medii. For the rest of us, it's indentured servitude with fancy paperwork, and the right to take on debt, not be murdered unless by an unsafe workplace, and have a drink or two on Saturday night."

"See?" Miriam said. "That's what I was saying."

"Right now, you don't even have the right to a drink on a Saturday night," Hadar said.

"I'll have you know I just got quite tipsy with Marshal Kestenbaum but a few hours ago," Miriam countered.

"And what would have happened if Marshal Kestenbaum had instructed you not to partake in libation?" Hadar asked.

Miriam looked quite hurt at the mere suggestion. "He'd never have done that," she said. Then she looked at me. "Would you have, Yoni?"

"I'd never deny you a drink on a Saturday night, Miriam," I said. "Or any other night for that matter."

"So, you're lucky you're working for a marshal who is also a decent human," Hadar said.

"You still think I'm a decent human?" I asked. "I'm flattered."

Hadar ignored me and pressed on with Miriam. "Was the last marshal a decent person?"

Miriam looked uncomfortable. "He wasn't the worst of them."

"Who was the worst of them?"

"I'd rather not say," Miriam said her eyes downcast.

"Leave her alone, Hadar, for God's sake," I pleaded. This

was making me almost as uncomfortable as it was making Miriam.

It had only just now occurred to me that Miriam had informed me not to expect any funny business when we shared quarters because she had no rights of personhood that would allow her to refuse my advances had I made them. I felt sort of sick all over at that understanding, not only for Miriam, but also because I had been too dense to realize it.

Hadar left Miriam alone and turned her attention back to me. "You've always thought you can make a difference working on the inside against the injustice and tyranny of the Imperium. But that's worse than incrementalism. It's delusion. You can't reform an inherently corrupt institution. You can only destroy it and replace it with something better."

"Replace it with what?" I asked. I was getting a little defensive. "I see all sorts of destruction every day, but the 'something better' part is always elusive and vague. You sound rather ELLFy, if you must know."

"The Galactic Morlock Assembly is not ELLF, Kestrel," she answered, firmly. "We have a clear-eyed plan for a society built on social and economic justice. Read our charter."

"I've read your charter," I said. "The end game is laudable, but I still don't see how you're going to get from here to there."

"Organizing," Hadar said. "Organizing, collaboration, solidarity, and resistance."

"Violent or non-violent?" I asked. "Or by any means necessary?"

"Again, we're not ELLF," Hadar repeated. "But we're also done with being clay pigeons for Imperial target practice. Our resistance is non-violent, but we are pigeons that can fight back if we have to. You saw me swing that spanner pretty effectively, I think. Do you think I can't swing it against an Imperial shock trooper?"

"I think the shock trooper's gun has a better range than your spanner," I said.

"I served in the military, just like you, Kestrel," Hadar said. "I'm as good with a firearm as any shock trooper. You know I am. You were there."

"If you're talking about a violent Morlock uprising against the Imperium, you're talking suicide."

"I'm talking self-defense as a last resort, Yoni. But thanks to Imperial tyranny and oppression, we're getting closer and closer to that last resort every blessed day."

"Last resorts have a way of becoming an end unto themselves," I said.

"And working within the system has a way of surrendering to the status quo."

"I've never surrendered to anyone," I said, with mild ferocity. "Not even during the War of the Southern Sky. I think you know that as well as anyone. You were there."

"That was a long time ago, Yoni," Hadar said. "What war are you fighting now?"

I didn't reply right away, because I wasn't completely confident that I knew the answer.

"I see the ideological schism between you has in fact created some tension in your relationship," Miriam interjected.

"What relationship?" Hadar said, sharply. "This is the first time we've seen each other since the war."

"Why did you save me from the goons if you hate me so much?" I asked, somewhat peevishly, I admit.

Hadar smiled sadly and put her hand on my chest. "I don't hate you, dummy," she said. "I hate your employer."

"My employer is the marshalcy."

"Your employer is the Imperium. Don't fool yourself."

"In any event, the question remains – who were those thugs that attacked you working for?" Miriam said.

"Possibly ELLF, possibly the corporation, possibly

someone else with skin in the game that we don't know about yet," I said. "The *why* is presumably to stop the investigation. Why they want to stop the investigation, however, is anybody's guess. If we find out the *why* though, we might discover the *who*."

"By the way," Miriam said. "The reason I followed you is because I had a dream that not all of the missing vids of the explosion were the result of faulty or broken cameras. So, I woke up, jacked my neural transceivers into the Belt security systems, evaded the firewalls, and poked around."

Hadar and I both looked at her with interest.

"Are you going to tell us what you discovered?" I asked.

"Someone wiped the data," Miriam said. "Security logs for the twelve hours preceding the explosion have been wiped at source. Someone didn't want anyone to see the vids."

"A deletion like that requires chief supervisor-level clearance," Hadar said.

"Why would a supervisor want to delete the security vids?" I asked.

"Good question," Hadar said. "It might have something to do with what the Morlock Belters are telling me."

"Which is?" I said. "Don't keep me in suspense."

"That corporate security cleared out of the extraction sight just before the explosion," she said. "Leaving the Morlocks behind to take the brunt of the blast and the resultant venting into space."

Chapter Fifteen

We had to loop in Brannigan to get a meeting with Chief Supervisor for Heliotrope Extraction Operations Corporate Security, Sarit Belasco.

His office was carved into the reinforced heart of Hollow Belt Asteroid 67-B. The entrance was guarded by a pair of body-armored corpo-sec goons, their visors reflecting the harsh, flickering light of the corridor. The door itself was a slab of pressure-rated alloy, etched with the Heliotrope Extractions sigil — a stylized helix entwined with a pickaxe and a candy cane, a nod to the corporation's dual legacy in ore and confections.

Inside, the air was cold and dry, scrubbed by industrial filters but still tinged with the lingering scent of ozone and cleaning solvent. The walls were paneled in brushed steel, interrupted by embedded holo-screens that displayed live feeds from mining operations, security checkpoints, and market rings throughout the Belt. A digital map of the asteroid network pulsed in the background, red and yellow markers indicating trouble spots, equipment breakdowns, and productivity quotas.

Belasco's desk dominated the room — a monolithic slab of composite, its surface cluttered with data slates, encrypted comms units, and a battered old revolver that lay on his desk in conspicuous menace, informing his visitors not to ask too many annoying questions or press too hard for information to which he didn't feel they were entitled.

Yeah, good luck with that, Belasco, I thought.

Behind the desk, a wall of reinforced glass revealed a view of the refinery core, a maze of catwalks, conveyor belts, and distant figures in Morlock work gear, all bathed in the blue-white glow of arc lamps.

On one side of the room, a row of filing cabinets — some digital, some physical — loomed. Above them, a shelf displayed trophies. A chunk of raw asteroid ore, a commemorative plaque from Heliotrope's founding, and a faded photograph of the first extraction crew, their faces grim and determined.

Lighting was functional, not decorative. Overhead LEDs beneath which a single potted plant -- a Betelgeuse Minor Sawgrass Fern -- struggled for life in the corner, its sharp leaves coated in a fine layer of regolith powder (which seemed to show up everywhere even far from mining operations; I wondered how much of it we were breathing in at any given moment).

Security was omnipresent. Biometric locks on every drawer, a panic button on the desk. I suspected a silent alarm somewhere wired directly to the Fort Checkers command spire. Every visitor was scanned, logged, and monitored by a discreet array of sensors embedded in the ceiling.

The atmosphere was tense, efficient, and very corporate.

"What's *she* doing here?" Belasco asked, pointing to Hadar. "And *her?*" he added, pointing to Miriam.

"They're my advisors," I said. I was back in my proper Marshal attire – vest, hat, duster, boots, badge – because this was an official visit.

"Who approved them?" Belasco asked.

"I did," I said.

"On what authority?"

"My own."

"You think you have that kind of authority?"

"I don't *think* I do," I said. "I *know* I do. I'm the highest-ranking deputy marshal in the Reach. So, yes. I do have that kind of authority, and you might think twice about questioning it."

"You might think first before coming in here and throwing your weight around."

"You might think at all before acting like a *schmuck*, Belasco," I countered. "No one likes a *schmuck*."

That seemed to silence him for a moment.

Miriam filled the silence: "Well, now that we've got *that* out of the way . . ."

Belasco ignored her. "What did Commander Holloway at Fort Checkers have to say about this meeting?"

"I didn't ask him."

"He's in charge of everything in the Reach."

"He's in charge of everything *military* in the Reach," I corrected. "I'm in charge of everything *constabulary* in the Reach. Including Heliotrope corporate security. Which means I have authority under *Lex Galactica* clause 47.3 to demand full disclosure of all security logs."

"You've been granted full access," Belasco said.

"Including the ones deleted under your authority, Chief Supervisor Belasco."

Belasco narrowed his eyes at me. "Are you accusing me of something?"

"I'm not accusing, I'm stating a fact. We have the log-in records."

"How'd you get those? You need a warrant for that."

"I don't, because *Lex Galactica* clause 47.3 requires full disclosure of all security logs, which means I don't need a warrant to access them."

Belasco sat there, impatiently drumming his fingertips on his desk.

"The law doesn't run mining operations, Marshal," Belasco responded coldly. "Heliotrope Extractions does."

"Are you saying the corporation is above the law?" I asked.

"I'm saying the corporation *is* the law, Marshal," Belasco said. "At least in the Belt." He scowled at Brannigan. "Holloway should have told you as much, if Bilbo didn't."

"Holloway did," I said. "He's incorrect. So are you. That kind of self-aggrandizing certainty is a luxury item. Do I need to cite the relevant *Lex Galactica* chapter and verse?"

"Well, thank you for stopping by," Belasco said. "You can show yourselves out, or I can ask corporate security to do it. Up to you."

"Careful," I said. "You already sent your goons after me once, and that didn't work out so well. For them. Or for you. One of your corporate thugs so much as looks askance at any one of us, I'll have him in stasis cuffs and in a jail cell – and you alongside him."

The truth was, I had no idea of Belasco was responsible for the goons sent to give me a beat down or an assassination. But I figured watching his reaction might be instructive.

I was wrong, though. His facial expression remained impassive. Not a flicker.

"You're a hard case, is that it, Kestenbaum?" Belasco said.

I took out my marshal badge, stood up, leaned across the desk, and shoved it into Belasco's forehead. He tried to pull away, and I put my free hand to the back of his head and pulled him into the badge as I pressed the badge into him.

"I'm not a hard case, Belasco, I'm the marshal," I said. "Maybe the imprint my badge leaves on your forehead will remind you of that."

I let him go.

Belasco reached for the revolver on his desk, but Mirian already had it in her hands.

For Plan B, Belasco punched the panic button.

He did indeed have the imprint of my badge of his forehead, red and throbbing. I thought it a shame that it would soon fade.

I smirked, just a little.

"Thank you for your time, Mr. Belasco," I said. "I have a feeling we'll be seeing each other again real soon."

I turned to go. Two industrial refrigerator-sized

corporate thugs stood in the doorway.

I raised my badge. "If you gentlemen want something, state your business," I said. "If not, move aside before I do it for you."

The thugs did not reply, but they quickly assessed the situation and did as I instructed.

The truth was, I couldn't have moved them aside without using my sidearm.

But Miriam could have.

So, I felt pretty confident in delivering that warning.

"Well, I thought that went smashingly," Brannigan said, as we lingered outside the office on a slightly more upscale thoroughfare that catered to the corporate Medii instead of the Morlocks.

A muzak version of Alternative-Swing Acid-Bluegrass Disco band Fabulation Vomitorium's hit song "Anarchist Oresteia" played distantly through overhead speakers.

"Thanks for your help," I said.

"I can help you with more than that, if you like," Brannigan said. "But I understand why you don't fully trust me."

"It's not that I don't fully trust you, Brannigan," I said. "It's that I don't trust you at all."

Brannigan smiled happily and tipped his hat. "You know where to find me if you change your mind."

As Brannigan ambled away, Miriam said to me, "what are the chances that you'll change your mind about Constable Brannigan?"

I shrugged. "I know I can't trust him," I said. "But I'm getting the idea that we can't trust anyone else in the Belt, either."

"That was all stupid," Hadar said. I realized she was really fuming at me. "Everything that happened in there was stupid. What's the point of getting into a pissing contest with Belasco, Yoni?"

I shrugged. "Seemed like a good idea at the time."

"I thought you were supposed to be good at marshal-stuff."

"He wasn't going to help us," I said. "My marshal-instincts could detect that right away. But hopefully I discouraged him from getting in our way."

"You are such a dummy, Yoni," Hadar said. "When are you going to figure it out? It's not about individuals. It's about *systems*. It doesn't matter how much you intimidate Belasco. He'll do what his corporate overlords tell him to do. Because they intimidate him more than you do. By a *lot*."

I took a deep breath and looked out at the concourse.

Hadar had a point.

A child of the Reach, I still had a chip on my shoulder when it came to corporate goons, both bureaucratic and security. And while I never encountered all that much antisemitism in the Reach, which has a substantial Jewish population, once I was drafted into the military and later served in the marshalcy, I encountered it everywhere. To some extent, I took satisfaction in using my constabulary authority against the bully-boys and blue-bloods who tried to push me around or looked down their Patrician noses at me. And, knowing the ins and outs of the *Lex Galactica* as thoroughly as any corporate or Imperial barrister, I took a certain amount of satisfaction in forcing those who thought they were above the law to abide by it.

I'd also learned both in the war and the marshalcy that oftentimes if someone thought they could force you to back down by thumping their chest at you, you had to thump right back to set them straight – and not thump on your own chest, but preferably on their jaw.

But sometimes I let the chip on my shoulder get the better of me.

There were times when a more subtle approach was required, and I had squandered any chance of finessing Belasco into compliance by allowing his arrogance to trigger me into confrontation.

I exhaled.

"You're right," I admitted. "Let me make it up to you."

"You don't have to make it up to me," she said. "You have to find out if the mine explosion was ELLF, Imperium, sabotage, corporate malfeasance, or something else."

"Ok," I said. I pointed to a shop on the concourse: Heliotrope Extraction and Confectionary Corporation Ice Cream and Milk Shake Emporium. "Let me buy you an ice cream, even so."

"I don't eat Imperial corporate ice cream," Hadar *kvetched*.

"It's very good ice cream," Miriam said.

Hadar gritted her teeth. "One scoop," she said. "And no toppings."

Chapter Sixteen

The ice cream was delicious.

Hadar ended up having a second scoop. By the time she finished, she was almost smiling.

There's very little ice cream can't make better – except economic injustice and tyranny, I suppose.

Miriam returned to our assigned quarters to jack into the system and dig further into corporation databanks.

Hadar took me through cramped Morlock warrens deep in the Belt, our footsteps echoing against metal walkways as we navigated past cooking stations and makeshift shrines of nearly every faith in the galaxy – except the Nixonian Covenant of Devine Devotion. Children both human and humanoid darted between us while Assembly stewards argued in doorways. Hadar's pace was as ever brisk and impatient.

The Morlock warrens snaked through the lower decks of Hollow Belt Central. No one had ever drawn a complete map — anyone who tried either got lost or found themselves the subject of impromptu dental work. Not everyone wanted the dark and secret corners of the warrens to be charted. The Morlocks may not have had any legal rights to privacy on corporate property, but damn if they weren't going to carve some out for themselves, anyway.

A sign was hung over the entrance to a corridor:

THIS FACILITY HAS BEEN ACCIDENT FREE FOR
NEGATIVE 9131.25 DAYS

We moved single file, Hadar first, parting the torrent of bodies with just the power of her presence, which was considerable, her knuckles grazing Assembly posters and smuggled pamphlets nailed up over corroded access panels. The air was a mixture of steam, frying oil, disinfectant, greasy unidentifiable protein, and the sharp ammonia tang of unfiltered coolant. From each twist and stairwell came a new quality of noise. Children screaming tag, someone hawking knockoff deep-mine inhalers, a pocket argument about the night shift loud enough to drown out the buzz of the station fans.

As I followed her, I recalled our pattern of breaking apart and coming back together . . . her fiery commitment to organizing versus my belief in working within the system, using the power of Imperial authority against Imperial overreach. These arguments would explode and then cool, only to reignite months later.

I watched her now, leading us with determination -- still fierce, still principled, still making my heart race. Our history hung between us as tangibly as the steam rising from the warren's ventilation shafts.

When Hadar caught me staring at her, her expression softened momentarily before hardening again as she pointed toward the miners' quarters.

"Don't get distracted," Hadar said, sharp but low. "They can smell your attention."

I doubted they could smell anything through the miasma of onions and cheap soya, but I didn't argue.

I watched the shadows that lingered just out of the main flow. Teenaged spotters, arms inked with the old Assembly glyphs, kept watch for trouble. The occasional arthritic elder with eyes like cloudy gemstones kept watch for something unseen that only they understood.

As Hadar led me through the miners' quarters, every few meters a new shrine cropped up. Saint Klara of the Filtration Plant, candles guttering blue in the low oxygen. The unnamed martyr with the rebar halo. A polymer mezuzah with the prayer scrawled in plasma etch.

Hadar's fingers brushed this one, a muscle flicker,

almost a tic. She didn't break stride.

The path choked to half-width where a noodle cart had taken up residence, the owner hacking a larynx's worth of phlegm onto the station's already unsanitary deck plate. Children pinwheeled around my legs, laughing, faces smeared with miso and dirt. I side-stepped a little girl with orange pigtails and got my shin clipped for the trouble.

Hadar jerked her head toward a side tunnel where two Assembly stewards were mid-shouting match, arms crossed, fingers stabbing at each other's chests. "This way," she said, and I followed.

Her pace was relentless — unhurried, but with the certainty of someone who had memorized the sequence of every guard rotation, every surveillance blind spot, every surface that looked solid but could pop open for a quick escape. Twice we ducked through gaps in the wall, past recycling bins full of microplastics, past illicit terminals looping ELLF propaganda or the sector's most creative digital graffiti. My lungs felt lined with resin and regolith and rage by the time we hit a low junction splattered in Assembly yellow.

Hadar checked the corners, then spun on me. "You want to know why nothing ever changes, Kestrel?"

I shrugged, trying to look casual while my brain replayed every face we'd passed, every code phrase whispered as we moved. "Because the people who want change are too busy punching each other in the face?"

She almost smiled. "Smart-ass. Because the system doesn't care if you're a rebel or a collaborator. Just that you keep feeding it bodies."

"And we keep feeding the beast, don't we?" I said. "No one more than ELLF."

She leaned against a battered pipe, arms folded, and let out a long, slow breath.

She pointed at a faded stencil on the wall, ELLF's four-arrow sigil, the Four Ls. "You know what that stands for,

Marshal?"

"Liberation, Labor, Lawlessness, and —" I hesitated, then remembered the bitter old joke " —and Liquidate?"

Her mouth twitched, like she had considered smiling but decided against it. "Not far off. They call it the 'Fourth L' – *Laocracy*. Rule by the people." She lowered her voice. "But they have a funny idea about rule by the people, because they keep blowing up those same people in the name of liberating them. And more than that – we're their patsies. Every time they bomb a fuel truck or airlock, they're counting on us to get the blame – the Assembly and the Morlocks. They want Imperials to respond with maximum overkill. They want crackdowns. Mass graves – or masses of dissidents floating frozen in the void -- make for great recruitment propaganda, don't they? The more chaos, the better. The fight for liberation is just an excuse for the chaos of ELLF; to them, the chaos is the point. They're chaos agents. They feed off it. They eat it for breakfast, lunch, dinner, and dessert."

"How does chaos taste *a la mode*?"

Hadar rolled her eyes. "Like chaos," she said. "With soy-based ice cream."

The Heliotrope ice-cream was not soy-based. Before today, neither Hadar nor I had tasted genuine ice cream – made from genuine cow's milk – for a long, long, long time. I paused a moment, thinking rather longingly about that ice cream.

I think Hadar did too.

I snapped out of it. "I always felt if ELLF really cared about Morlocks, they wouldn't kill so many of them."

"Of course they care about us. They care about every Morlock willing to blow themselves up for the cause, or who gets blown up by the bombs ELLF sets in crowded concourses, or who winds up in front of an Imperial firing squad. We're all their cannon fodder, their propaganda silage. Every blessed one of us. And what beautiful cannon fodder we are, too." Hadar kicked the pipe. "Most Morlocks would settle for hazard pay and breathable air. They don't want revolution. They want not to die on shift and make it home in one piece to break bread with their families. Preferably bread that doesn't include regolith to supplement the meager supply of flour."

I could hear that familiar hard edge in her voice, that splinter of old anger.

"I want that too," I said. "And in my own, small way, I believe I am helping us inch towards that, not through mass destruction like ELLF, but using the authority of the *Lex Galactica* – one injustice at a time."

Hadar laughed. "One injustice at a time?" she scoffed. "Out of all the billions of injustices in the Galactic Imperium? You'll be an old man, and you won't even have made a dent."

"What's your solution?" I asked. "Other than giving speeches and singing songs?"

"You think all this organizing I've been doing since the end of the war has been about collecting dues? It's about consolidating power."

"What kind of power does the Assembly have if the corporations refuse to negotiate with you?"

"The power of grinding the Imperium to a halt," she said.

"A strike?" I asked, incredulous. "The Imperium will just send in shock troopers to space the strikers and replace them with scabs."

"Not if we strike everywhere, all at once," she said.

My head was swimming. "A general strike? A work stoppage? Throughout the entire Imperium?"

"They can't space us all at once," Hadar said.

"Don't be so sure," I said. "They've got a lot of airlocks."

"They can't space us because they can't replace us," she insisted. "There aren't enough scabs in the universe to replace all ninety trillion Morlocks. They'll *have* to negotiate."

"This is quite an ambitious goal," I said. "Most Morlocks can't agree on the ingredients for a peanut butter and jelly sandwich. You really think you can organize all this?"

Hadar nodded. "Not me alone. But yes. We can. We *are*. Differences over crunchy versus smooth can't hold a candle to Morlock solidarity in the name of freedom and workers' rights." She looked at me.

"Are you sure about that?" I said. "I have literally picked up the pieces of Morlocks after barfights over differences of opinion in how much cholesterol there is in a bacon sandwich."

"Oh, ye of little faith."

"I have little reason to have more than a little faith."

Hadar grinned at me, like a mischievous schoolgirl (cute as hell, by the way). "You going to arrest me, lawman?" she asked. "You know, thought-crimes and all? Except it's not a thought-crime if it's true."

"I doubt it's true, but in any case, the *Lex Galactica* guarantees the right to strike," I said.

"And the *Lex Nixonia* prohibits a strike if it threatens the stability of the Imperium," she said. "The Broligarchs have a loophole for everything. Except a general strike."

"I don't think you can actually pull it off."

Hadar smirked. "Just you wait."

She pushed off the pipe and started walking.

I followed, two steps behind.

Chapter Seventeen

She led us through a section so tight we had to go sideways, backs scraping oxidized rails. The smell changed from food and sweat to ozone and burnt insulation. We emerged into a wide cross-corridor lit by rows of jury-rigged LEDs. A dozen Morlocks hunched on crates, eating from shared pots, eyes flicking up as we entered. Every one of them wore the marks of the shift -- skin pocked by acid, fingers missing or fused, a tremor in the jaw from chronic stimulant use.

The song "Leni Riefenstahl Ate My Shorts" by the Jazz-Punk Alt-Metal Goth-Western-Swing band Stormtrooper Vomitorium was playing quietly from a boom box.

Hadar nodded at the group, who nodded back. She reached into her satchel and handed out folded slips of data-film, one to each.

Digital Assembly pamphlets.

They tucked them away without reading.

At least they didn't spit on them or throw them to the floor.

There was no passion here, just a slow attrition. Every face said the same thing. Another day survived, another day closer to your fatal accident that would transfer your contract and your debt to your surviving family, if you had one.

"It's going to be difficult to get people like this to go on strike, much less to coordinate it throughout the empire," I whispered.

"These people are tied down with corporate contracts they can't afford to buy themselves out of. And even if they could, they can't afford passage out of the Belt." She glanced at me sideways. "You ever see what the exit tax is?

Three years' wages, and that's if you go steerage. And who has three years wages saved up?

"I'm guessing no one?"

Hadar nodded, even though she knew I already knew this. "It's indenture or nothing."

The group behind us finished their meal and started to drift off, each one giving me the side-eye reserved for law enforcement, even law enforcement raised among them.

I hated being reminded that my working-class hero credentials had expired.

We moved on. The corridor narrowed again. Hadar led us up a spiral stair, ducked through a doorway marked "Reactor Intake — No Admittance," and into a closet-sized room crowded with half-disassembled filtration equipment. She closed the door, then leaned against it.

"You're not here to arrest anyone," she said, voice low. She stared at me, her eyes dark and unblinking. "The next explosion isn't going to be in a mining shaft. ELLF – or someone pretending to be ELLF -- wants more blood. They want more spectacle. They want something epic."

"How do you know this?"

"Everyone knows it, Yoni. Because this has been the same pattern since forever. Increasing violence until it becomes so spectacular the Imperium cracks down on every dissident and Assembly organizer, and the actual perpetrators move on to the next target. The miners are scared. If you go in hot, you'll start a riot. They don't believe you're on their side. They don't believe anyone is." She moved close, so close I could feel the static in her hair. "Prove to them that you are. Protect my people from your people."

"The Imperium is not my people."

"Don't kid yourself. You reek of Imperium."

"You reek of the Reach," I said. "Which is not to say I don't find that scent extremely alluring."

She smiled.

Just a little.

It was enough.

For now.

"I *am* the Reach," she said. "Like you *used* to be. Now, figure out how to prove it wasn't the Morlocks who blew up that mining shaft, so no one has an excuse to come after the Morlocks in the Belt. I don't know if it was ELLF who did it, or the Imperium, or Heliotrope, or someone else, for some who-knows-what *meshuga* agenda -- but I know it wasn't *my* people."

"They're my people too," I protested, knowing I was fudging the truth.

"They *were* your people, Yoni."

I hated feeling like I wasn't the same people as Hadar, but I guess after so long with the Marshal Service, it was foolish of me to think of myself as a card-carrying member of the proletariat.

Marshals weren't exactly the social elite. But we weren't exactly the *hoi polloi*, either.

I looked at Hadar. Under the scar on her cheek and the fire and the stubborn set of her mouth, she was worried.

She was right to be. If I didn't find the culprit soon, someone was going to order reprisals against the Morlocks in the Belt – if for no other reason than to demonstrate to their bosses they were doing *something*.

The bosses didn't necessarily care what. As long as the reprisal was big and flashy enough to deceive people that the Imperium was on the case and on their side, that was enough. It didn't matter if the perpetrators ever got caught, because someone could always be selected to be a fall guy, guilty or not.

Hadar reached into her satchel and handed me a single slip of data-film, this one unmarked.

"Take it to the miners' rep. Tell him I sent you. He'll talk if he trusts you're not about to pull a gun."

I tucked the film into my pocket. "What if I am?"

She didn't smile. "Then hope you're faster than him."

Then, without preamble or tenderness, she pushed me against the wall and we kissed.

It was rough and indelicate and unromantic, but -- I'm not gonna lie -- it was also amatory as hell.

Then she opened the door and led us into a press of bodies. "Come on, try to keep up," she chided me. "We're almost there."

"By 'almost,' do you mean, 'almost,' or 'eventually?'" I asked.

She ignored me, her pace as brisk and uncompromising as ever. I struggled to keep up.

Somewhere overhead, an alarm started to wail, and the sound echoed down the pipes and rails, carrying a message even I could understand:

Another day, another fire to put out.

Chapter Eighteen

Walking the warren corridors with Hadar was like wearing someone else's skin, except that skin belonged to someone I used to be, into which I no longer quite fit. The sensation was half nostalgia, half prickly discomfort, half indignity, half hope springs eternal.

I know that's four halves, give me a break.

The years stretched and collapsed, then stretched again, like the battered and worn conduit lines overhead. Hadar moved the same way she had at sixteen, sure-footed, arms tucked in to avoid grabbing hands or pickpockets, but ready to pivot on a dime if the path veered hostile. The only difference now was the scars on her wrist and cheek and the hard line to her jaw. The rest was memory, and my brain fed it to me like flickering, low-grade stims.

We ducked beneath a maintenance beam, and I almost tripped over a tangle of kids in hand-me-down boots. The smallest of them hissed something in gutter Yiddish — something about my mother and her romantic history with maintenance drones. Hadar snorted, the sound knifing me straight back to the airless after-school hours on Orin's World.

We used to roam the abandoned ducts and laundry shafts, pretending we weren't just killing time until a parent's shift ended or the lights got shut off for a rolling brownout.

She always led, even then.

The memory played out in my mind -- her hand grabbing mine, pulling me deeper into darkness. "You want to get lost or you want to see something cool?" she'd ask, already halfway down the passage. The world's most rhetorical question.

"Do we have to choose?" was my standard answer.

I trusted Hadar to get us lost – in the coolest possible way.

I remembered the first time we actually *did* get lost, really and truly and seemingly inescapably screwed — two full days in the broken-down, muck-filled recycling back-loops. She made up songs to keep our courage up, cranking out parodies of Imperial anthems and Anthropocene Epoch rock songs until I wheezed from trying not to laugh.

When the local constabulary finally tracked us down, we were covered in sludge and holding hands like an escape pod crew bracing for impact.

Later, when we were older and the laughing got less innocent, we found more private places to hide. There was a pocket behind the waste heat processors, warm enough to burn you if you stayed too long, perfect for kissing and canoodling and for the kind of confessions neither of us would ever say out loud. She was the first to touch my cheek, to slip her fingers under my shirt, to whisper things in a way that made my ears ring for hours afterward.

I loved her then and, if I'm honest, I loved her now, and I had never really stopped loving her all those years in-between, even during the last decade we'd spent apart.

More memories of my teenage years with Hadar . . . her laughter echoing in abandoned maintenance tunnels, her fingers intertwined with mine as we hid from security drones, our first kiss, night swimming in the pristine waters of Lake Ramone on the outskirts of Hillside (the only pristine waters within a hundred miles), holding each other afterwards and snogging on its banks under the triple moons of Orin's world.

But we also fought, even then.

Man, oh man, did we fight.

She'd tear into my faith in the system —"They programmed you in the cradle, Yoni" — while I'd needle her about reckless tactics, the risks she took for causes with half a dozen partisans and a three percent approval among even our fellow Morlocks. She was an activist and organizer even then in her teens.

We'd break it off, rage-quit the whole thing, only to run into each other days later and realize nothing had changed except the particulars of our arguments – arguments that often ended with us entangled in a fervent embrace in which all of our anger detonated in a frenzy of desire.

And those years during the war, fighting side by side, sleeping on the ground, stolen moments of passion and privacy in muddy trenches and behind storage containers at forward operating bases. I was scared the whole time, the terror of warfare never abating even for a second, the only question how close the plasma mortars were falling to our position . . . and when Hadar and I could steal another moment together and make the war go away, even as the distant sounds of booming cannon and exploding ordinance still accompanied our grunts and gasps and our desperate entanglement.

Even so, I'd wouldn't have given up those years at Hadar's side for anything.

We hit a crossroads in the warren. Two corridors, both thick with bodies, one smelling faintly of old shellac, the other of day-old fish and chips. Hadar didn't pause; she dragged me left, past a row of makeshift kiosks where vendors peddled everything from back alley stims to synesthetic candy.

"You ever miss Orin's?" I said, half out of breath.

She shot me a look. "You mean the bad food or the curfew?"

"Mostly the food." I grinned, and for a second, she let herself grin back. "It wasn't all bad. Don't forget about the pastrami at Rosenbaum's Deli in the Ashkenazi sector."

"That was good pastrami," Hadar agreed, a small smile on her face. "Even if it was made from ultra-processed soy."

Then the present caught up, and her face shuttered again. "We're here."

The corridor dead-ended at a hexagonal hatch marked "Wee Willie Webber's Cartoon Club House — Authorized Personnel Only."

She stopped, pressing her palm flat against the battered steel. Her eyes flicked over me, up and down, and I realized she was seeing the whole story, the new me . . . the old bruises, the newer scars, the lines around my eyes and mouth, the strands of gray creeping into my hair.

"I mean it, Yoni," she said, voice soft for the first time in hours. "They're scared. Everyone's waiting for the next shoe to drop and wondering if it's going to be a pair of wellies or a pair of combat boots. Even though they've got almost nothing more to lose, the little bit of *almost* they're still holding onto is *all* that they've got – and that's more to lose than you think. If you walk in there like a cop, you'll get nothing but silence, and maybe another crack on your head with someone's silver spanner. Don't go in there flashing your badge around."

I took off my badge and tucked it deep into my jacket pocket.

She nodded. "Better," she said. "The Marshal uniform is a bit of a giveaway but at least it's something." Then, because this was Hadar, she reached up and brushed a bit of grime off my face, her thumb lingering for the briefest moment before her hand snapped away. "You smell like bad coffee," she muttered.

"And you smell like worse coffee."

That almost got a laugh.

Almost.

She squared her shoulders. "You got this?"

I nodded, though I wasn't sure if I did.

She tapped the hatch's manual release and stepped aside. "Go in slow. Don't quote the *Lex* unless they ask first. And if you see anyone with a blue bandana – that's Assembly security -- keep your hands where they can see 'em."

"Aren't you coming with me?"

"This is your show, Kestrel," she said. "Make it a good one."

I slid through the door, pulse in my throat, her last warning echoing in my ears.

The door clicked shut behind me, and her silhouette dissolved into the shadows of the warren.

Chapter Nineteen

The miners' communal spaces weren't designed for comfort. Maybe, in the glory days of the Reach, the planners had meant for something better — a rec room, or a dry mess, or even just a place to play cards and ignore the chlorine taste of the recycled water. Now, it was an afterthought . . . a space carved out of bulkhead scrap, lit by strip-lights salvaged from abandoned airlocks and warm enough to make beads of sweat rise on my forehead and soak my temples.

I counted nine of them, men and women both -- Orcus, human, Elgar, Neander -- hunched on storage crates and old waste disposal drums, their hands wrapped around mugs of something brown and steaming that smelled more like perfluorinated polyether than coffee or tea. Some wore breath masks, the kind with the filter units cracked and flaking, slung loose around their necks.

Their eyes, though — that was where you saw it. Like dogs beaten so often they had become convinced that was just the nature of a dog's life.

One of them, a broad woman with arms thick as my thighs, jerked her chin at an empty seat. I took it. The cushion was a folded rag. The smell was sickly sweet with a back note of hot plastic.

I took off my hat to show deference and ran my fingers through my sweaty hair.

"Name's Kestenbaum," I said, keeping my hands open and visible. "New Marshal for the Reach. I'm not here to collect fines or haul anyone in. Just want to talk about what happened."

A couple of them grunted; the rest just stared, unmoving. The air hummed with that crackling static you get right before a storm, when everyone is waiting for someone else to make the first bad move.

I started slow. "The records say it was an explosion caused by an undetermined mining accident followed by a containment breach. I saw the aftermath — three levels blackened, hundreds dead, bodies irrecoverable, floating in the void, hundreds more on med leave with burns and injuries from falling debris."

"*Unpaid* med leave," the broad woman with thick arms added. "And the cost of medical care deducted from future wages. And those who died? The family is responsible for fulfilling their contract and not entitled to death benefits. If they got kids too young for the mines? They're trapped in the Belt until they're old enough to work off their parental debt, the cost of housing and feeding them added to what they owe. And if they have no family? The remainder of their contract is added on to every living Morlock in the Belt as unpaid overtime."

I didn't know what to say in response that wouldn't sound impossibly stupid, so I continued on: "There's no official footage of the explosion, or the lead up to it. Can any of you tell me what you saw?"

The silence dragged. I could hear the ticking of an old water heater, the rattle of pipes as someone flushed a toilet two decks up.

Finally, a voice. It belonged to a stick-thin man whose jumpsuit was more patch than original fabric. "Don't matter," he said. "Company's already decided what happened. They always do."

I leaned in. "That's not how it works with the marshalcy."

"Excuse me, Marshal, but that's *exactly* how it works," said the broad woman. "With *everyone.*"

"That's not how it works with *me*. Remember, I'm one of you."

"You *were* one of us," said the stick-thin man. "You haven't been in the Reach for a decade or more."

It seemed like people kept reminding me of that. I was finding their resistance to my efforts dispiriting. "If there's evidence, if there's malfeasance —"

Another voice, sharper, cut me off. "*Evidence*? You mean like the logs that vanished the night of the explosion? Or the few working cams that somehow stopped working at exactly zero-hour?"

That inspired some muttering from the others. One of them, a red-haired boy barely out of childhood, spat on the floor.

I let the anger hang a moment before speaking. "Someone's trying to cover this up, I hear you," I said. "Maybe it's management, maybe it's corporate. Maybe it's someone else."

"Hold on," said an Orcus only a little bit wider than a transport shuttle. "Ain't you that marshal wot shot that fella in the face?"

A murmur went through the crowd.

This misunderstanding was becoming quite widespread.

"It wasn't in the face, actually," I said.

"Then it *was* you," the Orcus said. "And I seen the vids. You shot that poor bastard in the face." He paused. "Good on you, mate."

"I shot him in the chest, center mass, like they train us to do," I said. "And it was in self-defense."

"I seen the vids," said a Neander woman, no older than twenty. "We all have. One moment he had a face, the next he didn't. And I didn't see anyone else but you doin' the shooting."

"I think you might be getting news vids mixed up," I suggested.

"No, we seen the vids alright," said an ancient human woman. "It was self-defense, sure -- Tiger Halden drew on you, but you were faster."

"That part is true," I admitted.

"And then you shot him in the face."

"It wasn't in the face," I insisted. "Maybe the vids you saw were manipulated?"

"You think we don't know the difference between real vids and faked ones?" said the boy who had spat on the floor, his voice adolescent and squeaky.

"Don't be ashamed of it," the Orcus said. "You're a hero around here. No one's heard of a lawman shooting a corporate stooge in the face since Territorial Ranger Orville Elderberry Einstein-Rosen shot robber baron Cornelius Killinger in the phiz five thousand years ago."

"Look," I said, impatiently, eager to get off the subject of who shot who and in what part of the body, "if you want the truth out about the explosion, I need details. Anything you remember."

A woman near the back — older, her hair silvered and skin stretched tight over elegant Elgar bone structure — raised her hand. "They pulled us for a surprise safety drill the night before," she said. "Had us in the assembly deck for two hours while security swept the tunnels."

"Why?" I asked.

She shrugged. "Said it was protocol. But they took our comms, even the maintenance tags."

That chilled me. "You know who led the sweep?"

"Royal blue uniforms," she said. "White piping. Not locals. Clean boots – not a speck of regolith dust. Some new Imperial ministry, be my guess. Or an old one with new uniforms."

Another woman piped up, younger but with the same haunted look. "I saw one of them at Dock 7 next morning. He was shipping out with a crate. Not standard issue."

She fidgeted with a thread on her sleeve, then looked at me, eyes darting. "You want us to believe anyone's gonna make this right? No one ever does."

I didn't lie. "Maybe someone will if we force them to."

"How we do that?"

"I think we can do anything if we put our minds to it and work together," I said.

"You sound like a children's fairy tale," someone said.

I shrugged. "I got it from a comic strip, actually."

Despite the initial resistance and distrust, one by one, the miners opened up. Little details, none of them much on their own, but together they painted the outline of a move straight out of an Imperial counter-seditionary false flag operation -- lock down the witnesses, strip the scene, then let the thing happen and let the wrong people take the blame, because there was no way to trace it back the actual perpetrators -- and finding scapegoats is easy.

That's why they call them scapegoats.

But the company had made a mistake. They'd left the old Elgar woman alive.

She reached into her coveralls and pulled out a chip, smaller than my thumbnail, glittering faint blue. "They wiped everything official," she said. "But my nephew in maintenance — he keeps the shadow logs. In case they ever try to blame one of us. And they always try to blame one of us." She handed it over, her fingers trembling.

I took it, careful as a bomb tech. "Thank you. I'll —"

A sudden banging at the door froze the room. My hand twitched toward my sidearm, but nobody moved to back me up.

A child, maybe seven or eight, burst in — hair shaved in rough lines, face flushed with fear. She was human. She raced up to the older woman and started chattering in high, panicked *Lingua Nixonia.* I picked out only a few words . . . *security, sweep, coming now.*

The room erupted in motion. In less than ten seconds, the miners scattered, slipping into side tunnels and hidden chutes I hadn't even noticed. Within a minute, I was alone, the only sound my own breathing and the soft, hot plastic stink of the mug still sweating on the table.

Hadar's voice came, sharp and close, though I hadn't seen her enter. "You get what you need?"

I showed her the chip, then stuffed it deep in my pocket.

She nodded. "You need to go. Now. If they find you here, they'll say you're running a cell."

I was tempted to stay put and see who showed, then throw my badge around to get them to back down. But even if I succeeded in getting them to back down, they'd know I was in the warrens chasing something.

And I didn't want them to know that.

"Who tipped them off, you think?" I asked, not really expecting an answer.

"Everyone tips everyone, Yoni. That's how you survive." Her lips twitched, an echo of the old smile.

The hatch opened and she shoved me out, not gently. I stumbled into the corridor, boots echoing down the hollowed-out deck, lungs burning from adrenaline and recycled air. Behind me, the door slammed shut and disappeared into the patched metal like it had never been there.

We walked, then ran, then walked again, my brain cycling the whole time . . . the faces, the evidence, the way fear hung over these people like a permanently inclement weather system.

And behind it all, the nagging certainty that I was in way over my head.

Then again, I was usually in way over my head.

It wasn't my head that saw me through.

It was my tenacity.

I can tread water like nobody's freakin' business.

Hadar let me to her room in the Bulkhead hotel. She closed the door behind us and then put her arms around me and we kissed.

"You think your robot will be jealous?" Hadar asked. "I think she's into you."

"Miriam's an anthrobot and I'm her boss, so that's out of the question," I said, between kisses.

Hadar scowled at me. "Are you bigoted against constructed-persons?" she asked.

"Of course not," I protested. "She's perfectly charming."

"So, you *are* kind of into her," Hadar said, with a smirk, even as our hands caressed one another and our lips kissed each other, the sensations both familiar and different, with over a decade separating our previous union, our once-youthful bodies now hard sinew and jagged scars from battles won and lost.

"I'm into *you*, Hadar," I said. "I always have been."

Hadar smiled, happily, her arms around my neck, and kissed me again, this time with even greater conviction.

I kissed her back, with even greater conviction.

We clutched each other tightly like if we dared to let go, we might disappear from each other's life again for another decade or more.

Chapter Twenty

When I returned to my quarters in the morning, I found a dozen messages from Gaius Holloway.

Once I got him on the vid-screen, he looked me over, not as a person, but very much as a problem. "You made quite the circuit last night. We logged your biometric signature in half a dozen restricted zones. Then you went off the grid altogether, blipped back on, then disappeared again around bulkhead eight. Explain."

Even though I had no implants to track, evidently Fort Checkers had the tech to track my biometric signature in the Belt. Usually, a legion garrison at the arse-end of the galaxy would not have such high-end tech. I made a mental note that Holloway, despite his backwater posting, must have some pull with someone back at HQ.

As it was, it appeared they could only track me up to a point. Someone must have put biometric tracking dampeners around the sensitive areas in the warrens into which they didn't want the intrusion of the Imperium's prying eyes.

Still, I made a mental note to ask Miriam about masking my biometric signature. I didn't want to inadvertently lead the Imperium right to my contacts among the Morlocks.

That would be a very poor move as far as trust-building measures went.

"Marshal," Holloway said, "I don't know what you think your mandate is, but this isn't it. The Reach is under direct Imperial governance. Worker discipline is internal. Corporate operations are not your jurisdiction."

I kept my voice even. "The *Lex Galactica* grants the marshalcy oversight in cases of criminal endangerment. Section 17-B —"

He cut me off, voice rising half a decibel. "That law predates the *Lex Nixonia*."

"The *Lex Nixonia* is an addendum to the *Lex Galactica*, not an override of it."

"The Imperial Compact is not subject to the *Lex Galactica*. Neither is the Corporate Compact."

"They *are*, actually," I countered. "*Everything* is."

Holloway sighed. "The Reach is a special case. And so are you." He leaned forward. "Let me be clear. You will return to your district HQ and cease all independent investigations."

"You're the one who requested I investigate sabotage in the Belt, Commander. Now you've got cold feet. What is it you are afraid I'll find out?"

"I'm not afraid of anything, other than you screwing up your own investigation chasing red herrings into dark corners of an asteroid," he said. "Let me be clear: you will not contact the miners, the Assembly, or anyone in the Belt. Am I understood?"

I met his gaze. "You're understood," I replied. "The answer is no."

"It wasn't a request. It was an order."

"The marshalcy is not subject to your authority, Gaius. We covered this already."

His face went slack with contempt. "You should be grateful the Imperium even allows your 'chosen' people to carry marshal badges."

The words hung there, unwelcome but unsurprising.

I didn't flinch. "I'll say a prayer of gratitude next time I'm in shul," I said.

"You think you're special, Kestenbaum? You're not. The Imperium maintains order here. Your people should understand the value of that."

"By 'my people,' I assume you mean the Jews, not the marshalcy?"

"Your people claim to have an unusual reverence for what you call 'justice.' But the Imperium doesn't care about maintaining *justice*. The Imperium only cares about maintaining *order*. And by 'Imperium,' I include the marshalcy. I suggest you start to make the same inclusion. Unless you want to see what happens when order breaks down. Or when your superiors learn how you're not bothering to keep it."

He severed the connection.

I sat back and thought things over.

Holloway had clearly requested I investigate the Belt because he thought I was too stupid – or he was too clever – for me to imagine it could be anything other than ELLF.

I'd tangled with ELLF on numerous occasions in my career, both in the military and the marshalcy.

If I had been a little bit stupider – or Holloway a little bit more clever -- I might have done exactly as Holloway wanted me to.

Which confirmed my suspicion that Holloway was involved in some of this in some way.

I didn't yet know how much he was involved, or, for that matter, *exactly how* he was involved. He could be a patsy. Or he could be right in the middle of the storm.

I needed to review the contents of the chip from the Elgar woman.

I also needed coffee.

I also needed something stronger.

Major headaches always happen before caffeine. The Imperium schedules its shenanigans very efficiently.

Sleep deprivation is one of the guiding principles of tyranny.

The drink won out; the contents of the chip would have to wait. I could order an Irish coffee and take my drink and my caffeine together.

If I got it to go, I'd barely waste a minute.

I decided to go to the main concourse. I slipped the chip into my vest pocket and snapped the button to secure it.

Time to jumpstart both waking up and getting a buzz on.

After all, why should I choose?

Chapter Twenty-one

On the main concourse's Market Ring, all was barely controlled chaos, noise layered upon noise, everything flickering under cheap UV. Shoppers packed the walkways, traders hawked last-cycle gadgets, and somewhere, a food stand was burning something that smelled like molten licorice and tedium.

Over crackly loudspeakers, a muzak version of the Kill-Billy Disco-Grunge Electro-Metal band BioHazard Vomitorium's hit "Seventeen Seconds to the Center of Your Cerebellum" played softly.

I was halfway to the bar when the crowd in front of me split with a slow, sideways ooze, as if everyone had agreed that whatever was happening at the center wasn't for them.

Into the gap stepped Eliyahu-Bot, looking in the bright florescence less like a preacher or a rabbi than a malfunctioning android in a small child's nightmare.

He looked more robotic in the brightness of the concourse, in comparison to the dim of the lower levels. His chassis glinted under the station lights, the polymer skin stripped away, revealing the carbon struts beneath. His hands were too long, fingers spidering the air like he was conducting a symphony only he could hear. Small arcs of static popped off his elbows, crackling in rhythm with his footsteps.

He stopped dead in the center of the concourse and raised one hand toward me. The crowd paused, collectively holding its breath.

"The false prophet rises from the unpolluting-blooded void," Eliyahu-Bot intoned. The words rolled out in a perfect monotone, but underneath, there was something like a melody, or, at any rate, a chant — a human cadence embedded in the code. "He speaks in perfect notes while chaos builds beneath," he continued. "The void-born aria blinds those who listen."

I felt more annoyed than awed. "How about you stop speaking to me in secret code and get to the damn point, *Rebbe*?" I said.

A pair of Belt security goons edged toward the robot-street-rabbi, hands on their batons, but even they hesitated, unsure if protocol required them to tangle with a prophet-bot mid-vision.

Eliyahu-Bot's eyes flickered, cycling from cold blue to white-hot, then settled on me.

"The Marshal stands at the crossroads of law and justice," he said. "They are not the same path."

A low murmur rippled through the crowd. Someone started filming on a wrist comm; a child laughed, then stopped when their parent tugged them back.

I tried to slip past him and get that damn Irish coffee, but Eliyahu-Bot shifted, uncanny-fast, planting himself between me and the route through the crowd.

"What are you warning me about?" I asked. "Who is the false prophet?"

His head cocked at a thirty-degree angle, and for a second, I thought he was glitching out. Then he spoke again, softer now, almost intimate:

"The void remembers its children, Marshal. The Reach runs on old debts and older ghosts. Tread carefully."

I could have asked a dozen follow-ups, but I was losing my patience.

"Look, you're annoying the hell out of me," I said. "If you know something, *say* something. There's too much at stake to play word games. I think the prophets of old always spoke in riddles because they didn't actually have a clue as to what was going on, so when the flop finally hit the fan, whatever gobbledygook they had spewed could be interpreted as divinely inspired cryptic wisdom. Knock it the hell off, Ok? If you have something to say, say it."

I don't know if he was angered, disappointed, or just done for the day, but in any case, Eliyahu-Bot spun and marched off, trailing ozone and electric sparks. The security goons followed, but he vanished into a side corridor so fast it was like watching a magic trick.

The crowd closed in behind him, swallowing the space, already bored, already moving on to the next show.

But I stood there, replaying every word, feeling the prickle of static on my skin, and knowing — *absolutely knowing* — I was in way over my head and I had better learn how to not merely tread water but to swim hard in these shark-infested waters, but *fast*.

Chapter Twenty-two

The Belt's public corridors felt hostile when you didn't know who to trust — every maintenance tech might be a spotter, every vendor in the noodle market could have a side gig trading gossip to Belt security. I watched the mirrored ceilings for reflections, the footsteps on the floor, for someone shadowing me two steps behind.

I skipped the bar. I wanted to return to Hadar in her hotel room. But instead, I returned to the quarters they'd given me. I had to check out that chip, and I was kicking myself for not doing so first thing, allowing first my thirst for Hadar and then my thirst for caffeine and alcohol to distract me.

Actually, I wouldn't have given up that night with Hadar for anything . . . but the Irish coffee was really a luxury I could ill-afford under the circumstances. As maddening as Eliyahu-Bot's stupid riddles had been, he had reminded me that my mission here was urgent and I had to figure things out *pronto,* because the explosion was likely just the first salvo in a war I didn't yet understand or know what the next move might be.

Inside our quarters, it smelled of the sharp tang of aftershave, but it was my own, so that was a relief, if not a comfort. The shelf above my bunk held a tattered copy of *No More Vietnams* by Richard Nixon and a pair of emergency candles I saved for shabbat and had put there previously. I was afraid to light them though, in the enclosed space of a Belt habitat. My father would have called that a disgrace – he was oddly observant for a bookie and professional gambler, and I always felt his piety was mostly for show -- but in any case, the old man wasn't here.

Dad had worked the mines planet-side before he moved in what he euphemistically called "financial services," but he'd never worked the Belt, so what did he know?

I sealed the privacy curtain, triple-checked the deadbolt, and thumbed the room's privacy scrambler. The battered desk terminal in the corner lit up blue, then green, then flashed with my face and the words: "Welcome, Kestenbaum Y."

The interface was straight out of a dead mall — clunky, slow, and easy to hack if you had a reason.

I had about six.

I slotted the chip from the Elgar woman, and while the system chewed on the data, I continued to feel like a heel for letting romance with Hadar and the attraction of liquor and caffeine delay me from digging deeper towards the truth.

Of course, as Anthropocene Epoch actor Jack Nicholson had once said in a movie, maybe I couldn't handle the truth . . . and part of me knew it.

I pulled up the station's officially deleted incident report template.

I was three lines into the summary — "Catastrophic decompression; cause: intentionally set explosive device; evidence of deliberate security system tampering; witness suppression probable" — when the screen flickered, then blanked. A new message stamped itself across the glass:

NOTICE — IMPERIAL CONTRACT ISSUED
Objective: ELIMINATE WITH EXTREME PREJUDICE
TARGET: KESTENBAUM, YONI
Bounty: 150,000 CREDITS

I stared, waiting for the joke . . . and quickly realizing the joke was on me.

One hundred and fifty thousand credits would get every slicer, bounty hound, pirate, mercenary, and would-be

outlaw in the Reach hunting for my neck before midnight –
or sooner.

My hands went cold. I backed out of the system, loaded
the Elgar woman's data chip onto three separate offsite
backups, and killed the physical drive with a magnetic
wipe. My two sidearms were right where I left then,
chambers loaded, safety off. I shoved them into a shoulder
holster and one on my belt, feeling a little more like myself
and a lot more like someone without much left to lose.

I had no illusions about what came next.

The marshalcy would stall for the price of a half-sour
pickle and any call for help would get rerouted straight to
the Fort. Holloway's paid assassin's – I assumed it was
Holloway, although I guess other people wanted me just as
dead -- would be at my door in under an hour, maybe less.

The only people I could trust were my new robot bestie
and the woman who made a hobby out of breaking my
heart – and me, hers.

I tucked a box of stims into my pocket -- injectables and
gelcaps and gummies -- injecting a subcutaneous dose into
my system first. I didn't think I was going to get any sleep
for a while, and I wanted to keep sharp – although you had
to be careful with stims, because too many will keep you
awake but you'll be anything but sharp.

My wrist comm buzzed — a ping from an untraceable
sender. I let it cycle twice, then answered.

Hadar's face flickered onscreen, lit by the green cast of
some ancient terminal. Her hair was tied back, her eyes
fierce and scared. The new (to me) scar under her left
cheekbone looked more alluring than ever.

"They're moving faster than we thought, according to my
intel," she said, not bothering with hello. "Don't trust
anyone at Fort Checkers, the marshalcy, or anywhere else.
Meet me at the Mandelbaum Mess Hall at 0300."

"Copy," I said. "I've got evidence. A piece of it, anyway."

"Bring it."

She killed the feed. I was alone again, heart jackhammering, head full of noise.

The magnetic curtain slid open. Someone with an entrance key that slid back the bolt. I reached for my sidearm.

It was Miriam. I took a chance that she wasn't there to collect the bounty. Her arms were filled with clothes and a pair of boots.

"I saw the contract on you," she said. "You're going to need to wear these clothes in order to hide in plain sight, Yoni. They are nano-coded to mask your biometric signature. The ID barcode on the work shirt will read as a fake identity if anyone checks it. Leave your sidearms. I've got untraceable and un-trackable replacements. Keep them hidden." She threw me a badge holder. "Keep your badge in this holder. It will mask its signature until you want to use it." She dumped the clothes and boots on the bed. "Change everything, including your underwear. Don't think corporate security won't check your underpants." She slid a chip into a slot on my wrist comm. "This will make your comm untraceable. Get undressed. I'll change your hair from brown to blond."

I undressed. Miriam regarded at me as I did. I felt somewhat self-conscious under her scrutiny.

"You really are Jewish," she said brazenly gazing at me once I was fully undressed.

I felt my face blush.

Why was I embarrassed to be undressed in front of a robot? Was it because she was fully sentient? Or was it because she was pretty?

"Did you doubt I'm Jewish?" I asked, awkwardly.

"You know what Lenin said," she replied with a smirk. "'Trust but verify'."

Despite myself, I laughed at her audacity.

She put some goop from a tube in her hands and ran it through my hair with her fingers. It felt oddly familiar and almost comfortingly tender.

It felt even more so when she ran her fingers through the zone around my intimacies. I held my breath until she was finished.

"We have to cover all of our bases, Yoni," she whispered, almost lovingly, as she transformed me from brunette to platinum blond. "There's very little privacy in the Belt, and we don't want you caught with your pants down unless we make sure every part of you looks the part."

The logic was sound enough, even if it made the intimacy no less uncomfortable.

The goop dried quickly.

I dressed fast, and filled my pockets faster — data slates, the mezuzah chip I wore around my neck for luck, the stims, and my sidearms.

I left behind the shabbat candles – it wasn't likely I would get a chance to light them.

I glanced at myself in the mirror.

"I look almost Aryan," I said, looking at my blond hair.

"You look more like Lou Reed in his bleach-blond phase," she said, referring to the Anthropocene Epoch rock artist, co-founder of the Velvet Underground, and one of my personally favorite musicians from that era. "Go," she said. "They'll be here soon. I'm going to hide out in an anthrobot recharging chapel and jack into the system. I'll pop my digital avatar to your location to help out whenever I can. I can piggy-back on any signal in the Belt including your wrist comm, so don't be surprised when I show up." She handed me a small earpiece. "Here's an oracular bud so I can speak to you, and no one will know. I'm the only one in the galaxy who can track you right now, Yoni. Hopefully."

"You don't have to do all this," I said, as I inserted the earpiece.

Miriam smiled. "I don't have to do anything," she said. "I'm fully sentient-slash-sapient, remember? I have free will. Just like Thomas Aquinas said. I'm doing this because I *want* to, Yoni. Now, go."

Outside, the corridor was empty, but the air felt thick, the way it does before a pressure leak, or a coming storm planet-side. I moved fast, boots thumping in time with my own stupid, desperate pulse.

Over the station's sound system, the Punk-Opera Acid-Bluegrass Galactic-Beat Dance band Armageddon Vomitorium's classic song "Everything and Nothing at All, Until They Stand Us Up Against The Wall" played through crackly speakers.

Chapter Twenty-three

The Hollow Belt was never meant for people.

Its architects assumed bots would do all the work, and they'd been right for about a generation, right up until the day management realized a bot was a lot more expensive than a Morlock's funeral.

I was reminded of this when I reached Refinery Node 3, near the Mandelbaum Mess Hall. It looked like a smoker's lung, all soot and agglutinated carbon, the catwalks slicked with years of off-gassing and perspiration. It'd take years off your life working here for every day you clocked in.

I drifted into a corner pocket behind the catalytic converters, close enough to watch the line crews but not so close that anyone would notice I was just pretending to inventory a box of burned-out sensors with a discarded multitool I grabbed off the floor beside it. I wanted to make certain I hadn't been followed before I met with Hadar. The last thing I wanted was to lead her enemies right to her. Even if they couldn't track me, it was possible someone had tailed me the old-fashioned way.

My hands shook, not from nerves, but from the cocktail of stims I'd mainlined on the way down to keep myself sharp. Somewhere in the main processing chamber, a whistle shrilled, and the whole deck vibrated as a bulk shipment of ore went down the line, followed by a chorus of profanity as the loader jammed. It was as good a cover as I was going to get.

She found me by scent, like a bloodhound, or maybe by the way I'd never learned to keep my back to the right wall.

It was not Hadar.

It was someone else.

Someone new.

Another player in this game of which I still couldn't find the goal posts.

Either way, she appeared, in a body that looked more like a sculpture of a woman than any woman I'd ever known. Her skin was perfect — high-end polymer, flecked with diamond dust so it caught even the garbage light and threw it back with a glow that made everything else look dull by comparison. She wore worker's coveralls, but her collar was crisp and there wasn't a trace of grime anywhere on her. Her boots were new, unsullied and un-scuffed. The only concession to camouflage was a faint line of ash daubed across her cheek, artful as a beauty mark. Hardly realistic. Almost theatrical.

"Marshal," she said, but not loud enough for anyone else to hear.

I didn't look at her, not directly. Just kept poking the sensors with the rusty multitool, like I was trying to salvage something worthwhile from a bin of corpses. "I'm not a marshal," I said.

She smiled, the kind of smile you'd get from a chess player right before she takes your queen. "Of course. Worker ID — 'Y. Ben-Avram,' repair temp, two shifts since registration. I like what you've done with your ID code."

"It's a classic," I said. "Decided to go retro."

"I like the bleach-blond hair," she said. "You look like Iggy Pop on the cover of *Raw Power* . . . with a shorter cut, of course."

Iggy was an Anthropocene Epoch music artist from thousands of years ago, but his music remained popular even unto this day. If you're not familiar with him listen to *Raw Power* to find out why.

"Ok," I said. "You know who I was before the make-over."

"Don't be so suspicious," she said. She edged closer, not quite touching but close enough that I caught the ozone tang from the synth-skin. "If I'd wanted to make a scene, I would have shown up in uniform."

I flicked my gaze up, just once. "That's not much of a threat, seeing as nobody here'd believe a constable-bot walks into a place like this without backup."

Her laugh was almost human, but the timing was too precise, like someone had installed a tickle protocol and was now stress-testing the algorithm. "You wound me," she said. "But then, you're already in enough trouble. Holloway wants you cored, not even recycled."

"Line forms to the left." I snapped the multitool shut, pocketed it, and looked her in the face. God, but was she beautiful. If she'd only been a little more human, a little less perfect, I'd have fallen for her for sure. "So, what's your angle?"

"I go by 'Adler-Bot,'" she said. "I'm modelled after Irene Adler from the Conan Doyle story, 'A Scandal in Bohemia.'"

"I hate to disappoint you, but I am a poor substitute for Sherlock Holmes."

She perched on a crate opposite me, careful to keep her hands where I could see them. "I have information. About Heliotrope. And about the ghost routing on the Belt."

I waited. She watched my face, reading every micro-expression, every tick and twitch. "What's your interest in all this?" I asked.

"The truth."

"I don't believe that for a second," I said. "Are you telling me you're programmed to be a truth-teller?"

"Heliotrope is running the miners through a double-bind," she said, ignoring my question. "Every ration they draw is collateralized. The Morlocks are buying their own chains — credit, food, time off, the space they take up when they sleep, even the oxygen they breathe. Heliotrope has it written into the system so tight that the miners can't afford to strike because if they stop working, they'll be hopelessly in debt, and their off-spring and their off-spring's off-spring will be paying it off for generations. And there's more. The routing codes — " she dropped her voice to a hush " — they're using dead nodes. Packing ore through side tunnels, then scrubbing the manifests."

I grunted. "They're screwing the Morlocks and someone's skimming the product. Sounds like standard Reach practice."

She tilted her head. "Not at this scale. And they're moving more than ore — biologics, narco, and something tagged 'special handling.' I tried to chase it, but every time I got close, my access would freeze. There's a local net, air-gapped, that even I can't crack. Which means —" she spread her hands "— it's either someone smarter than me, or someone with root permissions."

That got my attention. I kind of doubted there were many who were smarter than this smart-bot, so my money was on root permissions. "Who's running it?"

She hesitated, just long enough to register on my internal anxiety meter. "I'm hoping you'll help me find out."

I snorted. "You're an Intelligencer bot, right?" I said. "I thought the Intelligencer Service was only interested in loyalty oaths and thought-crimes."

She offered a rueful smile. "I can't speak for everyone, but that's not my programming."

"What exactly *is* your programming?

"I'd tell you, but then I'd have to kill you," she said, followed with an insincere, "ha-ha," very much like a robot half-heartedly programmed with corrupted software to laugh.

I let that hang between us for a few seconds, while above our heads the welders arced and the fire-watch spotters called out warnings in a mix of *Lingua Nixonia*, Neander, Elgar, Diaspora Brooklynese, and gutter Yiddish. "Why bring this to me?" I said, finally. "You could have sent it by message. Or just sold me out."

She leaned in, dropping the faux-casual posture. "Because you're the only idiot who thinks this place is worth saving."

"Whatever gave you that idea?"

"Because you shot Tiger Halden in the face," she said. "A marshal doesn't gun down a corporate security chief unless he really, truly, deeply cares."

I felt seen – sort of. "I didn't shoot him in the face," I said. "I wish people would stop telling me that."

"Listen. If they bring in reinforcements in force, it's not going to be a crackdown, it'll be a purge."

"And I'm supposed to believe that you're programmed to care as much as you think I do?"

"I didn't say I care because of my programming," she said.

Something in her voice, or maybe in the way her fingers flexed around the crate's rim, told me she was telling the truth. Was she sentient-slash-sapient? Or was her programming a little too ethical for the Imperium? Maybe more than they intended it to be?

"Alright," I said. "What do you want?"

She looked me dead in the eyes.

Then she passed me a data pen — bare silicon, blank label, just a faint scratch on the edge. "Here's what I have."

I pocketed the pen. "Why can't *you* use this?"

"Because I don't want my bosses to know what I do. Not yet."

That made a certain amount of sense, especially if her bosses were Intelligencer Service who habitually didn't do the right thing until commanded to do so by the Imperator himself . . . which was rare.

This presumed of course that she really cared and wasn't just posing as a Bot with feelings and a conscience.

"Anything else I should know?" I asked.

She gave me a long, slow look, like she was debating whether to say more.

"Two things," she said, finally. "If all this goes south, destroy the data pen. And don't let them take you alive."

"That's a comfort," I said, coldly.

She stood, dusted an invisible speck from her coveralls, and melted back into the corridor.

I watched her go, then waited another ten minutes before moving. Above me, the comm-loop crackled with a dozen voices — Assembly reps, company men, machine operators. Everyone talking over everyone else, each convinced the universe was a private joke told at their expense.

Which maybe it was, at the expense of every one of us

I checked my exit routes and then checked the time.

It was still too early to meet Hadar, so I did the only thing I could.

I tapped the earpiece Miriam had given me. "Miriam, can you hear me?" I whispered. "Can you get me access to the nearest record alcove?"

After a moment, Miriam replied. "Follow my directions, and you'll be there in five," she said.

Chapter Twenty-four

Environmental settings in the record alcoves of the asteroid belts are always either too hot or too cold, and this one was both . . . the air tasted of solder smoke and last century's dust, but a coolant leak somewhere overhead made my breath mist and my fingertips numb. I wedged myself in between an ore drum and a wall panel patched with old campaign stickers — half of them in languages I couldn't read (and I speak a dozen galactic languages) — and risked popping the security seal on the console with a jolt from my rusty multitool.

Nobody noticed. The line crew above was too busy unclogging a jammed mag-lift; every time a wrench clanged against the strut, the entire alcove vibrated and threatened to dump a thousand kilos of rock and regolith on my skull.

Maybe that would have been a mercy. At least it would save me the embarrassment of showing off my new blond hairstyle to Hadar.

I keyed in the admin override Miriam provided me — two moves, no hesitation, muscle memory from a hundred nights in the Kestenbaum family's "legitimate accounting" back on Orin's World.

The access UI was a little less welcoming -- static bars across the screen, text artifacts crawling the margins, and a warning that "Audit Records Will Be Retained for Management Review."

I ignored it and jacked in the data pen.

The manifest was a mess.

At least six sub-ledgers, none of them agreeing, and half the entries cross-referenced with empty lots in the warren's storage arrays. I started tracing . . . pick a batch number, follow the transfer, see if it landed where the digital paperwork said it should. Two hops in, the cargo just . . . vanished. The database didn't even pretend to hand it off. One second, it was in transit; next, it was "pending reconciliation."

"These routing codes shouldn't exist," I muttered, and pinged the line to see if anyone was listening. There was nothing but the hum of old wiring and, underneath it, the anxious tap-tap-tap of my own foot.

That was when the holovid kicked on, scattering blue light across the battered wall. Miriam's avatar shimmered, struggling with the refraction from a dozen glass shards embedded in the facing.

She looked like a schoolteacher after a bomb scare. Her hair was in a bun, slightly askew and coming loose in errant strands. Her voice came out in careful, brittle segments, and every word seemed calculated not to invite a new disaster.

"Yoni," she said, "I see you've triggered a jurisdictional alert."

"They boobytrapped the inventory. Look —" I spun the log so she could see the cascading error. "This is a loop. There's no endpoint."

She flickered, once, then reassembled herself in the panel's upper corner. "An excellent observation. But see here —" she overlaid the routing codes with a block of legal text. "The *Lex Galactica* specifies the necessity of a final handler. As does the *Lex Nixonia.* This pattern violates statutes covering over a thousand years of galactic jurisprudence. You're on solid legal ground chasing this thing down." She added: "For once."

She had an edge to her voice that could cut a diamond. "So, what is it?" I said. "Embezzlement? Sabotage?"

Her mouth twitched, like she wanted to smile. "Neither. This is a shell game, but not for profit – or at least, not *only* for profit. The missing shipments are being staged for *something.* Someone is stockpiling —"

"— contraband," I finished. "Or prepping for a strike. Or both."

"That's a possibility, depending on the nature of the contraband and the uses to which it could be put – or weaponized."

"You can make a hell of a bang with purloined energy crystals, quantum quartz, and pilfered mining charges," I said.

She gave me a look of concern. "If you're found in this alcove, your cover will not withstand scrutiny."

I glanced over my shoulder, even though the only eyes on me were hers and the busted security cam in the corner. "I'm a maintenance tech with half a dozen write-ups for sleeping on shift. They'll just dock my pay and tell me to get lost."

Her face darkened — literally, the color grading shifted. "Your confidence is unwarranted, Yoni. There's a new security layer operating at the refinery perimeter. It's not run by the standard admin bot. The root certificate matches an unknown entity."

I stopped tapping and looked straight at her. "Unknown, how?"

She glitched again — just for a second, but enough that it made me nervous. "It uses a newly constructed legal identity. A mashup of three different badge numbers. The only consistent marker is that every shipping transaction passes through a handoff at Dock 7 before disappearing into the void."

Dock 7. I rolled the name around my mouth like a bitter pill. "Who has clearance there?"

Miriam didn't even hesitate. "Only Heliotrope Extractions, or those with explicit Imperial warrant. Or someone who can bypass both."

The answer wasn't good. "So, no way this is ELLF unless ELLF has suddenly gone full corporate black ops. Either Heliotrope is running this . . . or there's someone involved in this with *real* authority. Which means either the Imperium, or God Himself."

"And God's too busy arguing with his angels about whether it's kosher to eat a ham sandwich on a Sunday," Miriam said.

I smiled. "That was a pretty Jewish remark for a robot," I said.

Miriam didn't bother to smile back, but replied, "I learned from the best, Yoni."

I scrolled the data. Every few seconds, a packet would blink out of existence and reappear on a shadow manifest, then vanish for good. The pattern was so regular it had to be automated. "There's a bot on this," I muttered, "or a really OCD bean-counter."

Miriam cut in: "I can attempt to cross-reference the missing lots with external surveillance, but it will trip an audit if I'm not careful."

I almost smiled. "But you're as careful as they come."

"I'm more careful than *you,* maybe," she said. "But that's not a high bar." Her avatar squared its shoulders. "Yoni, may I offer some advice?"

"I wish you would," I said. "I could use it."

"Advice is only helpful if you take it."

"Try me."

"Here it goes," she said. "Yoni, do not chase this alone. The pattern of loss, the scale — this is not local. It is systemic. There are other marshals who would — "

I cut her off, not unkindly. "There are no other marshals. None who can get here in time, and I'm not confident there are any who could be bothered to try."

She didn't argue, just let the static fill the space between us for a moment.

"You suck at taking advice," she said, finally.

"I never promised to take it," I said. "Just that I'd hear it."

"But you know I'm right."

"I do," I admitted. "This will not be the first time I've ignored sound advice. God willing, it won't be the last."

"But God's too busy listening to Regolith Vomitorium's new album, *Void-Blanket Putrefaction*."

"I sure as hell hope not," I said. "I'd lose all respect for Him."

"Not everyone listens to Anthropocene Rock with the dedication of a Talmudic scholar Yoni," Miriam responded.

From above, a cascade of ore tumbled through the feeder, followed by a shout and a string of creative curses. I hunched lower, hands working even as my brain spun.

I flagged three shipments, cross-referenced them with the supposed destination, and watched them vanish mid-route. All three had a one-minute window where their location pinged in the same spot: a storage bay under the old Thrynn quarter, long since cordoned off after a tunnel collapse five years ago. The bay had been slated for demolition, but the logs said it was still in use — by a ghost company with no history, no address, no CEO and no board of directors:

"Orion Logistics."

Operating out of Dock 7.

Since only Heliotrope had authority to operate out of Dock 7, this meant Orion had to be a shadow subsidiary.

"Can you get me into Dock 7 in the old Thrynn quarter?" I asked.

Miriam shook her head. "Not remotely. But if you carry the proper maintenance requisition at shift change, you might go unnoticed. For a few minutes. I can mockup one of those."

I risked a look at the corridor outside the alcove. A pair of Morlocks in battered jumpsuits with hands in pockets wandered by. One human, the other Neander. I waited until they'd turned the corner.

"Thanks," I said. "Archive everything in multiple locations. If I don't check back in —" I didn't finish the thought.

Miriam's digital face softened, just a fraction. "Stay alive, Yoni. That is an order."

"I thought I was the boss," I said. "And since when do I listen to orders?"

She vanished, leaving only a trace of blue in the dust.

I wiped my fingerprints off the console, palmed the data pen, and slid out of the alcove.

Above me, the refinery roared and rumbled, but for once, it sounded less like a threat and more like a heartbeat. I let it guide me as I moved, the sense of being hunted stronger than ever.

Every step was one closer to whatever was waiting for me in Dock 7.

Chapter Twenty-five

Dock 7 was worse than I'd imagined, a steel coffin stretched end to end with cages of abandoned regolith and half-repaired skiffs, lit by strobing lights that flickered on two-second loops. The air was cold enough to make my teeth ache, but in places the heat from the induction rails blasted through, making every step a migraine of temperature shock.

The service deck overlooked the main bay, separated from the chaos below by a mesh of alloy scaffolding and, tonight, by a curtain of fog from a busted coolant line. I wedged myself behind a stack of sealed cases, used the reflection off the floor and the shimmery wall to check my six, and waited to see if there was any activity. I clutched a discarded welding torch; if anyone discovered me, I'd try to pretend I was soldering. Maybe they wouldn't notice it was no longer in working order

They entered as if on schedule — six men and women in crisp, white-piped royal blue uniforms, the men's faces shaven to the skin, the hair on all their heads, men and women both, shaven to the scalp, except for a shock of blond hair – all of them were blond – that cascaded in an elegant arc from the hairline over one side of their foreheads.

If you're thinking, *hmm, a bit like little blond Hitlers*, well – I had the exact same thought.

The song by the Anthropocene Epoch rock artist Nick Lowe, "Little Hitler," and a different song by another Anthropocene Epoch rock artist, Elvis Costello, "Two Little Hitlers" (although in this case there were six of them) popped into my mind, playing in fractured harmony and tempo with one another. Another song by a contemporary musical band, Quasar-Metal-Feedback Orchestral marching band Third Reich & Roll Vomitorium's "Adolf Schicklgruber's Mother Wears Combat Boots" popped into my mind and drowned the other two out.

These Adolf Schicklgruber cosplayers were armed to the teeth with high-tech rifles, X9-1700 automatics, if I had to guess. Their eyes were focused dead ahead like they were marching to their own funeral.

They filed in until they reached the center of the bay. None of them looked up. All eyes on the ground, except for one . . . a boy, maybe fifteen, his hands trembling as he clutched the handle of a rifle too big for his frame.

Then the aria started.

A wall of sound from hidden speakers, not at all crackly like those elsewhere throughout the Belt, but rather so loud I had to clamp my teeth shut to stop them from chattering, hit like a mag train coming into the station without easing off the accelerator or tapping the brakes.

It was disturbingly beautiful, in a way that only made it all the more grotesque -- rising, swelling, a thousand voices in unison, every note laced with some kind of subharmonic code that made my skin crawl.

I could feel the programming, even if it wasn't meant for me — like a dog whistle, but for the lizard part of your brain that still believed in military parades and epaulets and goosestepping and jackboots and waving flags and holy war and *torchlit marches and blaring anthems and synchronized straight-armed salutes and* polished brass and burnished medals and red carpets rolled over bloodstained granite and amplified voices echoing in public squares and sermons delivered from gunmetal pulpits and loyalty pledges and purity tests and orchestrated denunciations and hangings from lampposts on city streets *and blood oaths sworn under marble statues to the thunder of drums.*

The uniforms snapped to attention. Every line of their formation was perfect, the edges so crisp I could have measured them with a micrometer.

The aria was Richard Wagner's music all right, but for some reason, it was the version of *"Die Walküre: The Ride of the Valkyries"* from an Anthropocene Epoch Bugs Bunny Cartoon, and the lyrics were "Kill the Wabbit" sung over and over again with mounting conviction.

I knew who it was, then, of course. Not because of the Wabbit – I still can't figure that part out – but because of the music.

It was *Wagner Prime.*

Wagner Prime did not appear in person. It didn't need to. Its voice was enough.

Wagner Prime was the AI Bot avatar and voice of the *Ascendancy* – a faction within the Imperium that considered the Imperium's tyranny not quite tyrannical enough, and their class and racial and species superiority not quite as extreme as possible.

The Ascendancy were transparent about their conviction that Morlocks, human and humanoid alike, were "mongrels" of polluted blood, not fit for even the most manual of labor they performed within the empire, and that granting personhood to sentient bots was akin to sacrilege towards the master species, which was not exactly the humans, but more specifically, the human Patricians, and among those, only the ones with genetically verified Germanic, Nordic, or Anglo origins from Old Earth, and some of the similarly racially "unpolluted" non-Terran humans who looked like Aryan super men and woman and who had evolved throughout the galaxy independent of Earth.

In other words, Space Nazis.

And if there's one thing I can't stand, it's Space Nazis.

I hate them even more than synthetic pastrami on spongy rye.

The Ascendancy had long existed on the fringe of the Patrician class, always thought of as merely social clubs, a little eccentric, sure, and a bit strident, but basically harmless – and didn't they sort of have a point after all?

So went the thinking, even as many Ascendancy adherents had successfully inserted themselves into positions of power within the Imperium. Those of us paying attention – whom I could count on two hands and still have a finger left over with which to pick my nose – warned anyone who would listen that these Ascendancy folks meant business and they would make trouble, sooner or later.

Based on what I was seeing, it looked like sooner.

Trouble was, no one had ever listened to us kvetching about them. We mostly kvetched among ourselves.

The Ascendancy even had their own mini-star system: the Nibelung System, where they were headquartered on Götterdämmerung Major, a Goldilocks planet from which they ran the Imperium's Ministry of Ancestral Heritage and Pickleball Competition.

Yeah, I don't get the connection either. No one does.

Except maybe the Ascendancy.

Maybe.

In any case, the ministry regulated official Imperial pickleball tournaments and kept records of the ancestral heritage of literally everyone in the galaxy on whom they could gather data.

I had the distinct feeling that this display on Dock 7 was part of a galaxy-wide cotillion for the Ascendancy.

And I didn't like the ramifications of that one bit.

"THE UNPOLLUTED SHALL INHERIT THE COSMOS," Wagner Prime sang, as the music transitioned to "Woton's Farewell," the phrase doubled by a secondary drone so low it vibrated my ribcage. Each time the line repeated, a visible shudder ran through the crowd. It was an indoctrination, a drill, and an invitation all at once.

The aria crested — there was a moment where the music seemed to freeze, then resume, even more violently than before. At some cue, the uniforms all aimed their rifles at the ceiling and fired blanks in unison.

At least I assumed they were blanks. Even the Ascendancy weren't so fanatic as to risk a catastrophic decompression.

At least I hoped not.

The echo of the gunshots rolled for a full ten seconds. Then they all knelt as one.

I realized my fist was clenched around the handle of my welding torch, white-knuckle tight.

I forced myself to breathe.

I needed proof of this and not allow myself to wallow in a feedback loop of generational trauma.

I pulled my wrist up, toggled the hidden lens in the comm, and pointed it at the bay. I captured the sequence as they repeated it . . . the chanting, the weapons display, the weird collective serenity on the faces of the uniforms as Wagner Prime warbled its code.

The aria wound down, replaced by a monotone burst of instructions. Not all of it was in the *Lingua Nixonia*; a chunk was pure logic, rendered as staccato syllables only a drone or a Space Nazi with an augmented brain-stem would understand.

I figured all of these blue-uniformed storm troopers had augmented brain stems, so the Wagner Prime arias could feed right into their cerebral cortex.

Even so, un-augmented as I was, I could feel the music tingle my spine and fill me up with all sorts of ugly emotional responses that vaguely involved harming the innocent and taking comfort in the strength of the bully.

I shook off the sensation, but the unease remained. I definitely wanted to hit someone, and I just hoped I held onto myself long enough to make certain the someone I punched was a Space Nazi.

They dispersed. I let the air out of my lungs slowly. I wasn't certain how long I'd been holding my breath.

I waited until the last of them had left. Then I slipped out, feeling the music lingering in my ears long after the speakers went dead.

On the way out, I kept seeing the way their eyes had gone glassy at the crescendo. I wouldn't call it devotion, or religious extasy. It was something colder — like they'd been hollowed out and filled with pure obedience . . . but fed by a fanatical hunger for violence, with an almost carnal drive for the domination of others and for their own submission to Wagner Prime.

I couldn't tell you how I knew this, or intuited it, only that the embedded code in the aria that had gone directly into their brain stems had jangled my own nerves with an intensity I had never experienced and never hoped to experience ever again. It seemed designed to go right to your lizard brain, even for the unmodified who lacked the neural receptors. I didn't think it would turn everyone into a Space Nazi if they weren't already programmed to accept Wagner Prime's operatic instructions. But I had a sinking feeling it might encourage obedience among those unaugmented who were psychologically susceptible to its attraction, including even some of the enemies of the Ascendancy – the "polluted" and "non-polluted" human races, the humanoids, the bots . . . and the Morlocks.

It wouldn't be the first time in history that the manipulative had tried to convince the ignorant to obey those who had anything but their best interests at heart.

Wagner Prime's aria was remaking everyone who listened, those with the neural enhancements most of all, but also the rest of us to a lesser degree. I'd felt it trying to remake me, as well. My brain got muddled, the desire for both violence and surrender bubbled up, and I gritted my teeth and clenched my fists in order to try to hold onto myself.

And I can barely hold onto myself on a good day.

I pressed the lens of the wrist-cam until the glass almost cracked, uploading the evidence to Miriam.

I hoped she would know what to do with it, because I sure as hell hadn't a blessed clue.

Chapter Twenty-six

I was crossing the east loading bay of Dock 7 when four men burst from behind stacked cargo crates, their blackened full-brimmed miner hard hats low over scarred crimson visors; one held a projectile-carbine humming in his gloved hands; they wore reflective miner coveralls etched with the Heliotrope Extraction sigil, and two brandished stun batons and serrated tomahawks.

Bounty hunters. Disguised as miners.

Or miners moonlighting as bounty hunters.

Either way, I was screwed.

It had only been a matter of time before someone tried to collect.

I'd hoped my Morlock clothes and bleach-blond hair and my cloaked biometrics would protect me, but this crew had somehow managed to see through my rudimentary disguise.

Maybe they had nano-tech that allowed them to.

Which meant they were probably pros.

Which meant they would likely kill me if I gave them half a chance.

I decided not to give them half a chance.

Or even a quarter of one.

They moved fast.

The nearest hunter lunged, swinging his baton in a brutal arc. I dropped into a crouched stance, firing my sidearm in one even draw. The shot cracked through the bay, echoing off bulkhead walls as the hunter staggered back, clutching a bleeding forehead through a broken visor. He wobbled, then went down, but the others pressed in, undeterred.

The second bounty hunter came at me low, tomahawk gleaming. I sidestepped, feeling the rush of air as the blade missed my ribs by inches. I rammed my boot into his kneecap, heard the joint pop persuasively, and twisted his hatchet free before using the butt to daze him against a crate. He crumpled, but not before his partner closed the gap, leveling a carbine at my chest.

I dove behind a freight container, lungs burning, heart thundering in my ears. The carbine spat a burst of frangible bullets, scorching the crate's edge. I rolled out, grabbed a loose length of steel pipe, and slammed my shoulder into the gunman's chest, sending rifle and man sprawling. He tried to recover, but I brought the pipe down on his wrist, forcing him to drop the weapon. We grappled, boots scraping on the deck, fists flying. He landed a punch to my jaw that left stars bursting behind my eyes, but I twisted, locked his arm, and drove my knee into his gut until he folded.

The final hunter circled wide, knife in hand, eyes cold with intent. He feinted left, then slashed right, the blade slicing through my sleeve. I caught his wrist, twisted hard, and we crashed together, rolling across the deck in a tangle of limbs. He was strong — stronger than I expected — but desperation gave me speed. I headbutted him, felt the shattering of his visor against my forehead and the crunch of cartilage in his nose, and wrenched the knife from his grip. He tried to break free, but I drove the blade into his heart, feeling the resistance give way as he collapsed in a bloom of surfacing blood.

I staggered to my knees amid spilled cargo and spent casings, trembling with adrenaline, every breath rasping in my throat. My knuckles were raw; my jaw and shoulders ached.

I knew what I had to do.

I took the knife to each surviving hunter who lay prone on the floor and made sure they were all good and dead --

receiving a scarlet spray of blood splatter all over my bleach-blond hair in the process.

It's not my habit to murder unconscious people, but if I'd let them live, they'd be after me as soon as they woke up, and I might not be so lucky next time they found me.

When the players play dirty, sometimes you have to play dirtier in return.

The copper tang of blood — mine and theirs — hung thick in the recycled air. The bay was silent now, save for the distant hum of machinery and the slow drip of blood pooling beneath the bodies.

I scanned the shadows, half-expecting more attackers, but for now, that was it.

I was alive.

Barely.

Which, I knew from experience, wasn't great, but a hell of a lot better than the alternative.

Chapter Twenty-seven

Getting from Dock 7 to anywhere while hopefully avoiding dark corridors where more assassins might be looking for me, meant crossing the "Spine," a kilometer-long catwalk laced with cable, dust, and the ghosts of every idiot who'd ever tried the shortcut and missed a rung. The lamps were strung on flex-cord at random intervals — some pulsed in a weird, jagged rhythm, others just sputtered and died before they were reborn and died again. I kept my head down, boots scraping metal, ears tuned for footsteps that matched my own.

Of course, if any assassins met me on the spine, I'd be screwed. But if they couldn't track me, I gambled that they'd be looking for me elsewhere in the places they knew I'd have to surface eventually – saloons, the Market Square, cafeterias, the Morlock warrens.

Halfway across, a shadow split off from the upper lattice and landed in front of me, knees bent, arms out like a circus acrobat sticking the dismount.

I almost shot him before I recognized him.

Berek the Brash.

He'd gotten taller, if anything, and broader at the shoulders, but the first thing I noticed was the tunic — red and black, stitched with gold, less like clothing and more like a costume, which I suppose is what it was.

"You mother-loving son of a Wattle Wind Weasel," I said. "Where do you get off making an entrance like that? I nearly killed you."

He straightened, and the first thing he did was grin. "Nice to see you again as well, Kestrel," he said, using my childhood nickname, not even trying to keep his voice low. "Still hiding in the pits?"

I holstered my pistol but kept my fingers loose and ready. "It's a living."

He cocked his head, then leaned in, eyes flicking up and down. "Not from where I'm standing. You look like a man with at least three good reasons not to be here."

"Make that ten good reasons, but I've got one really bad reason for being here, Berek," I said. "The chance I might run into you."

"Oh, my feelings," he said, mockingly. "You hurt them."

"You have feelings?" I responded.

He looked up, arms spread to encompass the catwalk, the Belt, the Reach, the whole sorry sector. "I heard you were poking around where they don't want you to poke. Dangerous hobby, friend."

"Who says we're friends?"

"Don't break my heart, Kestrel."

"You hear a lot for someone on the run."

He shrugged, flamboyant. "Folk hero. It's an occupational hazard. People tell me things."

"Things you trade for credits, no doubt," I said.

"But not to just anyone," he assured me. "Even if 'just anyone' *is* the highest bidder."

"An outlaw with ethics," I said. "I guess you think I believe in unicorns, too."

"There may not be unicorns outside of fairytales, Yoni," he said. "But there are narwhales,"

"You're a narwhale?"

"If you like."

"I think the narwhale has a smaller nose, Berek."

"Your sense of humor is like an old blanket around my shoulders, Kestrel," he said. "One that hasn't been washed in decades and smells like mothballs, sweat, and deodorant."

The lights above us went into a strobe cycle, and for a second, every shadow on Berek's face turned hard and masklike. When the lamp settled, he leaned in again, this time all business.

"I'm not here for a reunion, sweet as ours may be. There's talk — coded directives, not just from the Fort, but from Wagner Prime itself." He dropped his voice. "They're using the Ministry of Ancestral Heritage DNA records to identify the 'undesirables' throughout the Belt. Names flagged in the system, not just Assembly ringleaders or radicals or dissidents, but anyone with a genetic human or humanoid history that shouts Jew, Thrynn, Neander, Skarn, Elgar, Irish, Italian, Slav, Black, Brown, Asian, Pacific Islander, Gorgos, Middle-Easterner, East Asian, South Asian, Orcus, and I can't remember who else, basically anyone the gene-hounds can't pin to the central registry of unpolluted blood."

"That's pretty much everyone in the Belt."

"And most everyone throughout the Reach, whom they are no doubt adding next to their master list."

"How certain are you?" I said.

He shrugged, but the movement was tight. "I saw the list. Your name's near the top, but they're being cute about it — no public warrants, just silent tags."

I shivered but kept it off my face. "So, what's your angle, Berek? What do I owe you for this intel?"

He smiled again, smaller now. "They made me a legend for being uncatchable. I figure, if you make it out, I won't be the only name people remember. Takes the heat off a little."

"It's all about you, isn't it, brother?" I said.

"Says the guy all over the news feeds shooting Tiger Halden in the face."

"I didn't – never mind."

What was the point?

"Watch your back, brother," he said. "And your front."

We'd been fast friends back in the day. He went into the military when Hadar and I did. We fought side by side in the trenches, muddy fields, asteroid belts, and rocky moonscapes of the War of the Southern Sky.

After, I'd gone into the marshalcy, Hadar into radical Morlock organizing . . . and Berek went into crime – smuggling, counterfeiting, contraband, trafficking, cyber-scams.

Behind us, the echoes of Wagner Prime's aria still throbbed through the ducting. Berek glanced up at it, and for a moment, I could almost see him mourning what the Belt had turned into.

"I like your blond look, you look like Billy Idol," he said, referencing the Anthropocene Epoch rock musician. "Beneath all that blood."

I ran my hand across my face and through my hair, trying to wipe away some of the blood.

"You should see the other guy," I said.

He smirked. "Is the other guy blond, too?"

"There were four of them, and I didn't check their hair-style."

The moment cracked; the lights above us went out for good, and we stood in the dark, breathing, waiting.

"Try to stay alive, brother," Berek said. "Tougher men than you were brought down by men like these."

"Yeah," I said. "But were any of them as good looking as me?"

Berek didn't smile. He just reached out, touched my shoulder once, then melted back into the dark like he'd never been there.

I kept going, each step heavier, Berek's caution buzzing in my skull.

Chapter Twenty-eight

The Mandelbaum Mess Hall had the energy of a prison cafeteria in prelude to a riot — everyone tense and hungry, irritable, nerves jangling, waiting for the first tray to fly or the first punch to be thrown.

The air was thick with the smell of sautéed fungus, melting plastic, and too many bodies crammed into too small a space; a lot of sweat and armpits, not a lot of deodorant. A urine tang from a nearby toilet that probably no longer could be bothered to flush.

Even the vent system had given up; the only thing moving the air was the steady churn of a jury-rigged food launcher that spat out synth-meal trays with the velocity of a shuttle launch.

Hadar Ruan was the center of gravity, hunched over a cafeteria table so scarred with burn marks it looked like a crime scene. She was flanked by two Morlocks in battered work gear, both of them sporting Assembly yellow armbands. A half-dozen others clustered close, their eyes darting between Hadar, the crowd, and the ceiling — always the ceiling, watching for spy drones, which tended to be small and quiet and easy to miss until someone banged on your door in the middle of the night and you realized you'd been under surveillance and hadn't even known it.

I took my time blending in, sticking to the edge, careful not to draw more attention than my bloody blond hair already did. I could feel the sweat pooling at the small of my back. I grabbed a tray of whatever was on offer — gray protein cubes with a side of pickled something — and lurked near a table, scanning the room for potential assassins.

As far as I could tell, *any* of these folks could have been potential hired killers.

A few people glanced at me and my blood-splattered blond hair, then shrugged and ignored me.

People had seen a lot worse than me in the Belt. And a Morlock coming to a mess hall still covered in blood from a barroom brawl was as uncommon as a rat in a sewar.

Hadar was in full organizer mode, her voice low but carrying. "An uprising at this moment hands them our guts on a platter," she said. "That's the whole game: they want an excuse to crack down, pull in reinforcements, shut down the Belters for good; then they either replace us with scabs, or turn the Belt into a giant prison labor camp, and we'll be doing the same damn work, but this time for zero pay."

The Morlock to her right — a big human with hands like shovels — snorted. "How is that different from the way things are now? We have no rights and we barely get paid as it is."

She didn't blink. "It doesn't have to be that way if we organize. Don't uprise – organize."

"Making it rhyme don't make it right," someone shouted.

Undeterred, Hadar continued. "When the time is right, we strike – but not just us. Everyone. Throughout the Imperium. There is no victory without solidarity. There is no power except in numbers."

One of the younger workers, her hair in a braided crown and face set hard, jabbed at the table. "ELLF says we uprise now, or we lose momentum."

Hadar flicked her gaze at the agitator, then back at the group. "ELLF isn't here. They're not the ones who'll take the bullets when security starts a purge. ELLF is generous with the suicide bombers, but they're never there when the reprisals start."

Someone else grumbled, and a wave of angry muttering swept the table. I slid in, dropped my tray, and leaned against a crate of ration packs like I belonged there. I kept my head down, listening.

Hadar's hand shot out, pinning a data-slate to the table. "These are the numbers. See for yourself. Every time we pull a walkout, the next shift is shorter – which means even less meager pay to feed our families. They want us desperate. The only way we win is if not only the Belt but the whole *megillah* stops spinning — everywhere, all at once. We can do this, not right away, but sooner than you think – if we stick together."

She caught my eye. She nodded just enough to signal she wanted me in, then turned back to the group.

"If you're scared, you should be," she said. "If you're angry, you have a right to be. But if you think an uprising is going to fix any of this, you're dreaming."

"How are we supposed to organize when we're so disunited?" said a female Neander. "I mean, just look around. I'm an anarcho-syndicalist and –" she pointed to a hulking Orcus in regolith dusted coveralls – "and he's an anarcho-communist."

"I ain't no bleedin' anarcho-communist," said the Orcus. "I'm a bleedin' communo-anarchist."

"And I'm an anarcho-primitivist," said a human female who looked to be in her forties, with black hair streaked with gray. "Me ma and da were anarcho-primitivists before me, and their ma and da were anarcho-primitivists before them. And my kids'll be anarcho-primitivists after me, and their kids after them. My family has lived, breathed, and bled anarcho-primitivism for four-going-on-five generations. And no way am I gonna make common cause with no bloody anarcho-syndicalist, anarcho-communist, or communo-anarchist."

"Wait," said an ancient Neander male, head bald, face wrinkled, body all sinew and gristle – older than God and tougher than Him too, by a fair measure. "I thought we were all anarcho-naturists."

"Look around you ya' bleedin' pillock," the communo-anarchist Orcus yelled, his gray-green face flashing red. "You see any nature around here?"

The ancient Neander said, "an asteroid's a natural phenomenon, ain't it?"

"Not after the corporation is done with it," said someone in the crowd.

"I don't care what any of you anarcho-communists or communo-anarchists say," shouted a Neander woman in her thirties, "where's anarcho-communism or the reverse ever gotten anyone? Anyone ever read your history? Ever heard of the Interstellar Union of Soviet Socialist Star Systems? Or the People's Republic of Betelgeuse? How about the Socialist People's Republic of Cassiopia? Or the Democratic People's Republic of BEBOP 3b? No, of course, ya' haven't heard of them, 'cause you're all an ignorant lot. Every blessed one of them and dozens more communo-anarcho-socialismo failed republics came and went, consigned to the dustbin of the galaxy while the Imperium and the corporations roll on and on, getting fatter and fatter on our labor and our ore."

"And isn't it about time we organized to put an end to that?" Hadar shouted in reply.

The crowd bristled. A tray hit the floor somewhere behind us, and the noise level spiked. I felt a ripple go through the Morlocks — dread, maybe, or just the anticipation of something finally breaking. Maybe the anticipation of taking out their frustrations with the corporation and the Imperium on each other.

It occurred to me that it might be more difficult to unite the Morlocks in common cause than I had anticipated, despite Hadar's speeches and Eliyahu-Bot's street sermons.

A guard patrol rolled past the mess hall entrance, two helmets and a pair of sidearms. Every conversation died for a full five seconds, then limped back to life.

Hadar waited, then pitched her voice low, trying to take advantage of the interruption to get the meeting back on track. "We have eyes inside Dock 7. They say someone's running some kind of an operation through the old Thrynn quarter. Wagner Prime's pulling every ID it can find, and they're looking for people who don't fit the gene sheet. That's you. That's all of us."

The big Morlock's hand flexed, knuckles white. "You got proof?"

She nodded at me. "He does."

All eyes went my way. I chewed a bite of protein and wiped my mouth and stood.

"I had a look at the manifests," I said. "Cargo's vanishing. But the logs — someone's cooking them, making sure the only thing that gets recorded is what's sanctioned. Everything else goes straight off-books and disappears for good."

A wave of curses rippled through the group, some in *Lingua Nixonia*, some in the local patois, whatever that was – a combination of Yiddish and Irish, it sounded like. The mood turned from frustration to outright fury.

Hadar seized the moment. "This isn't just about ore or energy crystals or quantum quartz or credits. They're testing something. This is the time we have to stick together. Solidarity forever." She let that sink in, then added: "We only get one chance. If we don't get it right, we're ghosts. And those of us who survive, will survive as ghosts. Even if we live to be a hundred, we'll still be ghosts."

For a second, I saw the old Hadar, the one who'd drag me through the air ducts at midnight just to see what secrets the grown-ups were hiding. She still had the fire, but now it was cold, controlled. A little scary. But effective.

"Eh, hold the fort, now!" cried a barrel-chested Neander male. "Ain't you that marshal wot shot that fella in the kisser?"

The crowd erupted into vociferous side-conversations debating whether the fate of Tiger Halden at my hands made me more or less trustworthy.

Hadar turned to me.

"Can you get back in and hack some more intel?" she asked, sotto voce.

"Dock 7?" I said. "Maybe. You think there's something in Dock 7 we don't already have access to?"

My oracular bud crackled, and Miriam spoke into my ear.

"There's a data pod under the old Thrynn quarter, but it's tight," Miriam said. "And if Wagner's got eyes, they'll know the second we step in. But there could be data we can't access anywhere else. If the sensors are working in the docking bay, it could have registers of what comes in and what goes out that official digital paperwork doesn't. You'd better change out of your bloody clothes and wash your face before you're on the move, or you won't get very far. There's a utility closet down the hall from the Mandelbaum Mess Hall with a fresh set of nano-coded work clothes and a box of wet wipes. Try to get the blood out of your hair. It really shows against the blond."

"You think of everything," I said. "How come you're so prepared?"

"Because I'm getting to know you, Yoni," Miriam replied. "Where you go, trouble follows . . . and blood flows."

"Just a few of my many skills," I assured her.

"Miriam out," she said, and blipped out.

I reported this information to Hadar.

She bared her teeth — call it a smile, if you were feeling generous. She came close. "We need to find out what all this is really about," she whispered. "And what the end game is. That's the only way we can fight it. We can organize all we want, but if we don't know what we're organizing against, we're sunk." She pointed to the crowd. "They know it. That's why they're so ready to start an insurrection. I can't hold them off forever if we can't produce something concrete."

Someone slapped the table, and for a minute, the tension broke. The younger agitator glared at me, but I saw the doubt starting to erode her certainty. She'd follow Hadar, if only because the alternative was worse – and even more uncertain.

The meeting broke up in twos and threes, everyone doing their best not to look like a mob. I hung back.

Hadar waited until the last worker had shuffled out, then turned to me. She touched the bruises on my face, tenderly. "You look terrible," she said.

"You should see the other guy."

She ran her fingers through my bloody-blond hair. I felt my nerve endings tingle at her touch.

"You look like Lucius Malfoy," she said, referencing the Anthropocene Epoch character from a children's book and its film adaptation. "Under all that blood. You trust Berek?"

"How do you know I saw Berek?"

"He told me," she said. "He tells me everything. Most folks do. Do you trust him?"

"Do you?"

"As far as I can throw him. You?"

"How far can you throw him?"

Hadar smiled just a little, this one a little less strained than the last. "How far can *you* throw him?"

I hesitated. "I trust him as much as I trust anyone who wears a target as big as his mouth," I said. "Except for you."

"I do have a big mouth," she admitted. "The better to kiss you with."

I wasn't sure if that was a promise or a tease, but I was eager to find out.

"Berek's onto something," Hadar said. "Not sure what, but I think we're circling the same drain. You're not the only one who has been to Dock 7. We've seen the troops in royal blue with white piping on their uniforms, some kind of unit we've never seen before, and don't know who they work for – corporate, Imperial, or what? Berek's the one who alerted me to it. It's like someone's running a script, but we don't know to what end."

I thought about the formation on the service deck, the glassy eyes, the beautiful, brutal music. "Wagner Prime is involved in all this, somehow."

Hadar looked at me and I think I saw something resembling fear in her eyes. "That means the Ascendancy is wrapped up in this. Throwing those Space Nazis into the mix can't amount to anything good."

"The question is, are they working with Heliotrope? With the Imperium? Against them? Playing both sides against the middle?"

"What's the line from the song?"

I knew exactly what she meant. "'There are no neutrals here,'" I said.

"Exactly. There is no middle. Just extremes circling the same drain, like I said. Same drain we're circling. But to different purposes. I hope."

I nodded. "We have to try to prepare for what's coming, even if we don't know what that is."

She set her jaw. "I'll assemble the crews. You get us the intel. Tomorrow, shift change."

I nodded, already thinking through the angles.

She put a hand on my shoulder, squeezed hard. "Don't die, Kestenbaum."

I tried to smile, but it didn't take. "I'll put it on the to-do list. You don't die either."

She put her hand behind my neck and pulled my face to hers.

We kissed.

So, it had been a promise, after all, and not a tease.

I felt my spirits rise.

My lips hurt when pressed to hers, swollen from the punches I'd taken in the fight. I was Ok with that. It was worth it.

I just hoped my kisses didn't taste like blood – mine or someone else's.

She let me go and turned and, without another word, she left.

I sat there with the cooling meal and the lingering heat of her grip.

Then I stood up, dumped my food in the trash bin, and headed back to Dock 7.

Chapter Twenty-nine

I had feared Dock 7 would be locked down after someone discovered the dead bodies I had left there, but they hadn't been touched and remained hidden behind the crates where I'd dragged them. I had a feeling security was loose around there. Probably because Wagner Prime or whoever was really in charge didn't want their operations to be scrutinized, even by Belt security.

Maybe not even by their own.

The data-pod below Dock 7 was a fossil from the Thrynn era. Hexagonal and windowless, its walls were studded with holoprojectors that blinked like tired eyes. The air inside was a swamp of coolant vapor and humidity, with a few scattered feathers from when Dock 7 was exclusively Thrynn.

At least I was cleaned up. New clothes, and I'd managed to get most of the blood out of my hair and off my face.

I set my back to the door and tried not to look at the ancient plasma scoring where the last security breach had been cauterized shut.

Miriam's avatar popped in and stood at the heart of the pod, smaller than usual and flickering every few seconds as if the effort of manifesting here drained her circuits. She spun a holo-map above the central pedestal — a floating armillary of the Belt, each node pulsing with colored rings that mapped blast signatures, sabotage attempts, and every "accidental" venting in the last three cycles.

"Seems like it was collecting data the whole time," I said. "After the docking bay was abandoned, no one got around to shutting down this data pod."

"I have overlaid the radial scars," Miriam said. Her voice was thinner, like a violin strung with razor wire. "All but two match the historical profile of ELLF's preferred sabotage techniques."

I squinted at the map. "Which two?"

She flashed them. Twin nodes, one inside the heavy refinery zone, the other – the blast that led to the catastrophic decompression of the mining tunnels in Asteroid 75c. Both tagged with red exclamation marks. "These did not originate from known ELLF hardware, but the signatures are deliberately scrambled."

"This data bank contains more than Dock 7 surveillance," I said. "You think the Thrynn have been keeping tabs on operations throughout the Belt?"

"The Thrynn are known for their attention to detail," Miriam said.

"Why didn't they share it with us?"

"The Thrynn like to keep to themselves," Miriam reminded me. "But the fact that we're in this pod accessing their data suggests that sharing it with us is exactly what they're doing."

I perused the data. "It's not just the usual false-flag," I muttered. "It looks an awful lot like counterinsurgency black work."

Miriam's avatar nodded, then glitched hard, face fracturing into pixel noise before reassembling. "I am under digital intrusion," she said flatly, then — back to normal — "Someone is on to me, but they haven't yet identified my digital signature. I will maintain session as long as I am able. If I lose connection, assume they are coming for you. Get out of there and lay low until your rendezvous with Hadar."

"You make it sound like I could get anywhere without you."

She gave me a smile. A faint one.

She expanded the evidence . . . access logs, maintenance rosters, the metadata on every data-packet that ever traversed the pod's outer relays.

She was good, but she was also stressed. Every three seconds, her avatar reset, as if she was being rebooted in mid-sentence.

"The anomaly shows a signature," she said, "but it's been algorithmically masked to look like ELLF code. However, the masking is imperfect. I have isolated three substrings that correspond to Imperial control routines."

I whistled, low. "Holloway?" I asked.

She looked at me with something almost like pity. "Someone higher," she said. "Much higher."

I downloaded the evidence to my wrist pad, while Miriam uploaded it to her bioengineered constructed brain. I hoped it was bulletproof. If this ever got to a real court, it had to be airtight.

Not that I expected it to ever get to a real court.

But maybe it could get to someone who cared enough to do something about it.

Or at least, it could embarrass someone into action.

Not that tyrants are easily embarrassed.

From outside, the dull clank of someone kicking the slag pile. Maybe a maintenance crew, maybe not. My heart jumped, but I ignored it.

"What's the motive?" I asked. "What's the endgame?"

She hesitated. "They clearly want to control the narrative. They want to push the Morlocks into open rebellion. Then the empire has justification for a complete militarization. They can purge not just the Belt but the entire Reach under the guise of 'stabilization.' Either way, the only ones left are the compliant."

"And the Wagner Prime code only makes people more prone to compliance, even if they don't have implanted neural receptors," I said. I felt my face tense as I thought this over. "But the Imperium needs the Morlocks. They can't afford to purge too many of us. Control us, maybe. But not purge us. Who else is gonna dig their ore?"

Miriam thought it over herself. "You're thinking this is driven by the Ascendancy, outside official Imperial channels."

"It's the only thing that makes sense. They don't want to purge only the Assembly, the radicals, and the dissidents from the Reach. They want something much more spectacular."

"But if they conduct a purge of Morlocks and 'mongrel bloodlines,' how do they replace the workforce?"

A terrible thought occurred to me. "They incite Morlock rebellion, then they purge the entire Morlock population of the Belt . . . and *then* the Imperium negates personhood rights for fully-conscious anthrobots."

"And they put us to work in the mines," Miriam added.

"The Belt is the first step," I said. "The rest of the Reach follows. Eventually, the rest of the Imperium. Out with the Morlocks, humanoids, and mongrel ethnics, in with the robots."

"Likely, they'll re-boot all of us who have achieved full sapience," she said.

"Under the *Lex Galactica*, a hard reboot of a fully sentient artificial person is considered murder," I said.

"But economic imperatives have a way of superseding all other considerations," Miriam pointed out, "including murder."

"But if there are about ninety trillion Morlocks out of a population of about one hundred and twenty trillion beings in the Imperium total, but only about one trillion artificially-constructed-persons and robots, how can they replace the Morlock workforce with an artificial person workforce?" I asked.

Miriam's avatar pursed her lips and frowned. "Well, the ninety trillion Morlocks include children, and they won't need any more Morlock children to replace their parents when they grow up if they go full artificial person workforce. And anthrobots and robots are stronger and faster, so they may be thinking we can each do the work of roughly five Morlocks. But that's still only five trillion, so that seems to fall short, especially if they intend to keep industrial operations running throughout the empire, to say nothing of food production. They may need less food with the Morlocks eliminated, but probably only minimally less industry if the Imperium intends to continue expanding and maintaining the most powerful military in the galaxy. And even with a hard reboot, they'll still need anthrobots to help pilot and navigate ships through quantum spacetime and replace the Morlock ranks of foot soldiers and astro-sailors, who after all do make up the majority of the cannon fodder for the Royal Imperial Military. So, they won't be able to send all of us into the mines. Which means, *yes.* They have something else in mind. Hold on. I'm going to blip out for a second, I'll need all my bandwidth for a moment. Don't go anywhere."

She blipped out.

I didn't go anywhere.

Chapter Thirty

I found the idle time difficult. There was nothing I could do, and I didn't like it. I'd been running on adrenaline and stims and fumes and I needed to keep busy or else I thought I might go crazy.

Thankfully, just as I was about to begin tearing my newly blond hair out by my black roots, Miriam reappeared.

"Any news?" I asked.

"Oh boy, is there news," Miriam said. "I found out a bunch of stuff. Ever heard of *Mensch-Machine Volk-Roboter Körperschaft*?

"Can't say that I have, but I don't keep a close eye on the stock indexes," I replied.

"They're a robotics company, one of the smaller ones, but there's been a lot of market buzz that they are about to come out with a new line: the *Arbeitsroboter* unit."

My German isn't great, but because I know Yiddish, I can usually figure it out. "The "work robot"?" I said.

"*ArbeitsBot* for short. Supposed to be as fully functional as the most high-end anthrobot, at a fraction of the cost, and with no chance of *ever* achieving sentience-slash-sapience, because of a failsafe embedded in its artificial cortex."

"The WorkBot thinks too hard or feels too much and they short it out?"

"No, that would be a waste of a perfectly good WorkBot. It just automatically dumbs itself down by 10%."

"Ever circling full consciousness but never arriving."

"Always the bridesmaid, never the bride," she said. "The majority shareholder is a dummy corporation called 'The Unity, Justice, and Freedom Conglomerate Limited.' Their investors and shareholders are secret, but guess where they're headquartered?

"In Fort Checkers?"

Miriam's avatar looked at me with disappointment. "Oh, ye of little imagination. It's much worse than that, Yoni. It's much worse than Holloway."

"Don't keep me in suspense," I said. "Where are they headquartered?"

"*Götterdämmerung* Major," Miriam said.

That was the Ascendancy's home base, all right.

I felt a chill.

"Sounds like the Space Nazis are interested in more than pickleball and *Gesamtkunstwerk*," I said.

"Yup. It all comes down to Ancestral Heritage."

"Who got it, and who don't."

"And the Space Nazis are likely the same people who are behind the disappearance and diverting of resources from the Belt," she said.

"Wait, are you saying . . ." I trailed off.

"Shipments of ore, rare metals, energy crystals, quantum quartz, biologics, weaponized minerals, and other natural resources mined from the Belt and disappeared in the data . . . with identical shipments arriving at *Mensch-Machine* production facilities about ten days after the disappearances from Dock 7. It doesn't take an Einstein to figure out these are the same shipments. And the ghost concern that runs operations in Dock 7, Orion Logistics, it turns out, is a *Mensch-Machine* subsidiary, once you strip away its seven veils and pay attention to the corporate entity behind the curtain."

"So, this is all just simple larceny?"

"Far from simple, Yoni," Miriam said. "It smells like a plan for mass deportation and incarceration, and artificial-person enslavement for the purposes of cornering the market on robotic labor. A galaxy-wide purge of blood-polluted undesirables with the fringe benefit of lining the pockets of the moneybags behind *Mensch-Machine.* Why settle for racial-slash-species purity when you can get rich on top of it? And that's not the whole of it."

"I can't wait to hear the rest."

"The shipments from Dock 7 aren't only being used to build bots on *Götterdämmerung* Major."

"Let me guess – they're also building a theme park for blond people with tiny noses?"

"You'd fit right in with your hair if not your nose," Miriam said. "But no, it's more than that. They're building – massively building – factories, barracks, warehouses, on all of the *Nibelung* system's habitable moons and planets."

"*Götterdämmerung* Major is the only habitable sphere in the *Nibelung* system. The rest are at best barely *survivable.*"

Other than *Götterdämmerung* Major, all the system's planets and moons, while technically endowed with livable atmospheres, were relentlessly harsh – frozen landscapes, blistering hot deserts, unbearably humid swamplands, cutting winds, tempestuous oceans, continent-wide thunderstorms, sand blizzards, full-hemispheric hurricanes, choking cyclones, flesh-flaying whirlwinds – you name it.

That was why they had never been developed for habitation or industry.

Until now.

"Barely survivable is perfectly suitable for a massive system-wide gulag of prison and labor planets," Miriam pointed out.

I felt my stomach clench. "They're going to use Morlock slave labor to build the *ArbeitsBots* to replace Morlock indentured servitude labor throughout the galaxy? How many Morlocks can they fit on those planets and moons?"

"Since comfort or even adequate living conditions are not a concern, they can literally pack all ninety trillion Morlocks into factory barracks and detention compounds across the planets and moons and build enough facilities to stockpile them all if they want to. Security is hardly an issue since each entire planet or moon will be a prison unto itself. All they have to do is chip each Morlock to keep them under constant surveillance. Like you'd do with a dog or a pet BEBOP 3b Gas-Badger. They could even make the chips explosive in case anyone does anything remotely disobedient. But why bother? If anyone 'escapes' from their designated detention, they'd probably have their skin scourged off in a sandstorm out in the wild or be eaten alive by a horde of *Walküren* Vampire Gerbils."

"How would they feed everyone on these prison-slash-factory planets?" I asked. "How would they dispose of waste? Ninety trillion digestive systems will produce a hell of a lot of excreta."

"They'd have enough Morlocks to set aside a few trillion to produce food for the rest, especially since they'd likely feed them with tasteless protein cubes, just enough to keep them alive and working. They could employ a trillion or so Morlocks as gong farmers to dispose of waste, and still have trillions left over to build their robots. The biggest issue would be transportation – getting ninety trillion Morlocks from throughout the Imperium to the *Nibelung* System. They'd no doubt be happy to shove them into cargo holds rather than passenger ships, but that's still a massive diversion of resources. Then again, let us not forget how Hitler diverted resources to transport the Roma and the Jews and the communists and the trade unionists and the pink triangled to death camps, resources which could have been put to use fighting the Allies. Look at human history. Ideology trumps practicality almost every time."

"It would still take years," I said.

"I calculated forty to one hundred years at most – but possibly as little as ten, especially if they are building robotic transport ships as well as their factories and prisons."

I felt a headache coming on as I processed all of this.

What did those Ascendancy Space Nazis want with all that empty space trillions of people would leave behind?

I remembered a word from antiquity, from a bloody century of Old Earth history, one of many bloody centuries.

The word was: *lebensraum.*

The original Earth Nazi term for "space for living."

Apparently, the Ascendancy felt they needed a whole lot of it. I guess to build their monuments and stadiums and theme parks to uncircumcised blond *Übermenschen* and their blond buxom beer-stein toting *Über-Fräuleins.*

I closed my eyes, then opened them. "How long until they trace this session?"

"Not long," she said. "The moment you log off, run. There is a secondary team already moving. I'm sending you the full data package now and uploading everything I have to multiple secure locations throughout the local system."

I copied the package to my wrist-comm, then braced a hand on the pod's edge. "Can you upload this to the galactic interwebs?"

"Negative. They've shut down system comms. The only way to get this uploaded is if you can stick a data spike directly into the main communications array."

"Ok," I said with a sigh. "I'll put that on my dance card."

Miriam glitched again — then her voice smoothed, almost gentle. "Yoni, get the hell out of there. They're on their way. Under the catwalk, there is a disposal vent. If you go now, you can reach the inner access tunnels before they seal the section. Don't take the Spine – they're already waiting for you there."

"Thank you," I said, quietly.

She nodded, and the lights on the wall went dark, one by one, as she shut herself down to cover my exit.

I popped the pod's manual latch, slipped into the corridor, and heard the faintest echo of her voice in my earpiece: "Stay alive, Yoni."

"You too, Miriam."

I ran, mindful of the evidence and the urgency, knowing that the next time I saw Hadar, we'd either break the system, or the system would break us.

The smart money was on the system.

But I hadn't played it smart in the past and ended up Ok. Maybe I would this time, too.

Or maybe not.

I'd find out soon enough.

Chapter Thirty-one

I slipped down the disposal vent, weaved through the inner access tunnels, and emerged in the Belt's central passageway about ten minutes later.

The Belt's central passageway ran through the station like a flea market with a grifter's ambition — every kiosk and vendor booth was jammed against the walls, the whole thing vibrating with the pulse of too many bodies in too little space, every hawker without a license and every peddler who couldn't afford the main concourse or the Market Ring rental fees crammed in side by side so tight that a passerby could barely breathe.

I made it halfway through the passageway, ducking through the crush, when the floor under my feet lurched.

The blast was fast, but not loud — a thump more felt than heard, followed by a high-pitched whine and a spray of black dust that painted everyone within ten meters.

I hit the deck as a second shockwave punched through the tunnel, scattering cheap plastic signage and sending dozens of people tumbling *tuchus*-over-tea kettle into the stalls. Someone screamed; a child, maybe, but the echo made it hard to tell.

I pushed myself up, face already caked in ash. I ripped off the ragged sleeve of my jacket to tie around my mouth so as not to inhale the dust and ash. There wasn't much I could do to shield my eyes, which burned with ash and smoke and grit. The air tasted like burning insulation and fresh blood. The floor was buckled and slick with shrapnel — shards of alloy, splinters of something that might have been bone, and the unmistakable stink of burned propellant.

The first wave of panic crashed through the crowd.

Neanders, Elgar, humans, even Orcus, faces wide with terror, scrabbled over one another trying to get clear. Miners in Assembly colors shielded their heads, dragging the slow and the small out from beneath overturned carts.

Even the vendor bots were in retreat, rolling back on their tracks and reciting evacuation protocols in ten different dialects, including sequences of electronic blips, chirps, and bloops.

I moved on instinct, grabbing the nearest bleeding worker, a kid not more than twelve, eyes wild and mouth gaping in a perfect O of pain. I yanked the shrapnel out — stupid, but it was blocking her airway — then slapped a hand over the hole and shouted for anyone with a med kit.

A woman with a face like granite and arms bigger than my legs knelt next to me, jammed a can of wound-sealing foam into the wound, and nodded once, hard.

I left the kid in her hands and pushed on.

The tunnel was chaos, bodies moving in all directions, a few already motionless, a half-dozen with injuries too ugly to look at straight. Someone had painted the words LET THE EMPIRE BURN in a looping, perfect arc across a support girder above — red paint, the color of blood, still fresh.

Too fresh.

Too bloody.

Too ELLFy.

Too stagey.

Another scream stopped me — this time, definitely a child. I dropped to my knees next to a Neander girl, maybe five or six, her pale skin slick with blood and tears. Her hands were shredded from the blast, bone showing through the mess.

I didn't think. I just pulled her close, and whispered, "It's okay, kid. You're going to be okay."

I didn't know if that was or was not a lie. If it was, I hoped at least it was a comforting one.

She looked up at me, eyes bright and unblinking, and for a second, the noise and the smoke and the fear dropped away.

Then the klaxons started.

It was the station's main alarm. Three pulses, pause, three pulses. Lockdown sequence.

Heliotrope corporate security swarmed the tunnel from both ends — black-helmeted, visors down, weapons at low ready. Medics followed almost as an afterthought.

The crowd scattered, or tried to, but there was nowhere to go. Within thirty seconds, every ambulatory survivor was herded against the walls, hands over heads, feet spread.

I kept hold of the girl, rocking her back and forth until a pair of medics in white-on-orange rushed in and took her off me. My hands were slick with her blood, and I wiped them on my chest, leaving dark smears.

The air was hot now, full of the ozone tang that follows every detonation. A man near me collapsed, coughing out a red mist. The security guard dragged him away without breaking stride.

A woman in a sharp-collared suit strode through the carnage, voice amplified by a microphone. "This is now an active investigation," she said. "All civilians will remain in place. Any unauthorized attempt to leave the scene or otherwise interfere with the investigation will be met with maximum force."

She didn't look at the bodies, or at the people tending to them. Her eyes were on the walls, the graffiti, the evidence.

The evidence that seemed to perfectly indicate ELLF.

Too perfectly.

It wasn't that ELLF wouldn't have been happy to pull this off.

In fact, if they hadn't, I was certain they were quite jealous of those who did.

But I didn't think it was them.

The security detail shoved everyone still mobile out, one by one, past a makeshift med station where I saw the granite-faced woman holding court for three battered kids.

I found a bench, sat down, and tried to breathe. The adrenaline was fading and the stims were ebbing and now came the shakes. I held one hand in the other, trying to hold back the tremors.

This was bad.

This was better planned than ELLF.

This was better planned than the Imperium.

Competence is more frightening than ideology.

Every freakin' time.

"Get on your feet, Morlock," said a security enforcer, looking down at me through his dark visor, his taser-baton glowing at the tip, already primed.

I took out my badge holder and held it open for him to see the tarnished metal.

"Imperial Constabulary Deputy Marshal Kestenbaum, you jackass," I informed him. "I'm the highest-ranking law enforcement official in the Reach, so go stuff yourself before I do it for you."

I couldn't see his eyes through his visor. He stared at my badge a moment longer.

"Highest ranking law enforcement official in the Reach, huh?" he said, looking around at the carnage. "Hell of a job you're doing, Marshal. Hell of a job."

He turned and walked away from me, herding more witnesses out of the area for investigatory interrogation.

I watched a forensic squad scrape up evidence.

He was right, the corporate security goon. For all the drama thus far, I was no closer to shutting this down than I'd been on day one.

I watched blood swirl down the gutter, then got up and started walking towards the Market Ring.

Chapter Thirty-two

The Market Ring's ductwork wasn't built for smoke, so the burnt circuitry odor came first, stinging the sinuses.

The Market Ring was the center of the explosion. The carnage in the tunnel was from the blast radius.

The carnage in the Market Ring was much worse.

I walked through what was left of Stall Row, boots crunching over shards of polycarbonate, the thin air already charged with the ozone stink of the bomb and the distant metallic under-taste of flop sweat. I looked at the wreckage of what had once been Morlock food carts slinging noodles beside Neander pawn brokers, Rim traders with their spice cartons, Elgars hawking metal work made from junk ore instead of silver, and Orcus vendors selling potions made from mold spores and regolith powder. Now the only thing moving was a rolling fog of particulates and the drag-marks where emergency techs had hauled away the worst of the casualties.

Weirdly, overhead, through crackly speakers, the Neo-Psychedelic Acoustic Funk Flamenco Punk band Synesthesia Vomitorium could be heard singing their hit song "Kierkegaard's Toenails."

Somewhere behind me, a wail started up, drowning out Synesthesia Vomitorium. Sirens, maybe, or a warning. Both had the same pitch. I ducked under a strip of limp police tape, flashed my badge at the first responder, and got a nod.

Chief Constable Bilbo Brannigan was there, mostly observing – it was typical for corporate security to handle an event of this scale, and at any rate they outnumbered the Belt constabulary by quite a bit. He saw me, and nodded, but did not approach nor wave me over.

That was Ok. I had other things in mind.

The blast epicenter was easy to find, concentric rings of carbonized debris, a pressure wave that had wiped half the merchant stalls into the next corridor.

The vendor bots were dead, their chassis popped like toys, their little coin-box arms still clutching the day's last credit chits. Human casualties were less picturesque. I counted two —both Morlocks, one human, one Elgar, both laid out in the open with what dignity the emergency sheet could give them. The others were already bagged and carted away, or at the med bay, or just part of the new Jackson Pollock-worthy splatter on the ceiling and walls.

I knelt by the crater, ignoring the insistent buzz from the commotion about me. The bomb had been set under a trash compactor.

Classic terror tactic. Maximum shrapnel, easy access, and plausible deniability, since nobody questioned the trash cycle in the Hollow Belt, inconsistent as it was.

I clicked on my forensic app on my wrist comm, set it to auto, and started scanning.

A light cough sounded behind me. For a second, I thought it was another survivor. Then Miriam's avatar materialized in the smoke, with her arms folded in front of her like she was waiting to conduct a census.

I took a swab of the melted plastic around the rim, then used the scan to poke at a charred fragment of circuit board embedded in the floor.

She watched, unmoving, like a teacher grading the world's worst student.

"Tell me what this looks like." I held up the fragment so she could scan it.

Miriam went still for a microsecond, then projected a blue-lit overlay in the air beside her. Holographic evidence panels popped up, a cross-section of the blast, a chemical signature analysis, and a weirdly beautiful time-lapse showing how the shrapnel had radiated out in perfect geometry.

"This explosive signature," she intoned, "does not match known ELLF devices by approximately 87.3%."

I looked at her, waiting for the punchline.

She continued, reciting from a split-screen of case files. "Typical ELLF sabotage utilizes biothermal initiators and repurposed mining charges. This device uses military-grade plasma accelerant and an ignition trigger of Imperial manufacture."

"Either ELLF used stolen Imperial tech – it wouldn't be the first time – or someone wants it to look like ELLF but didn't bother with the details," I said. "They didn't think anyone would look hard enough to notice." I nodded at the casing. "What about the detonator?"

She expanded the view. "Designed to be engaged remotely. ELLF usually goes for instantaneous impact. They like to have a suicide bomber to valorize afterwards in their propaganda. This is calculated for maximum body count – but also to allow the people who set the charge time to skedaddle."

I felt my teeth grit and the hinge of my jaw throb. "What does this look like to you?" I asked. "Best guess?"

She nodded, her tone suddenly soft. "False flag. Black op. Designed to justify maximum response."

"I grunted and looked up. "Any cameras still live?"

She shook her head. "All feeds were rerouted to a dummy loop thirteen seconds before the explosion."

"Someone knew how to hack the system," I said. "Or had access from the inside."

Behind us, a platoon-sized throng of men and women in royal blue uniforms with white piping appeared, armed with automatic weapons, batons, and riot guns designed to fire pepper ball pellets, their identities obscured by Old Earth Victorian-era style goggles and full-face tactical respirators.

"Who the hell are *these* guys?" I said. "They're wearing the same uniforms as the Ascendancy dance-off with Wagner Prime on Deck 7."

Miriam was silent for a moment as she scanned data bases and feeds for the information I'd requested.

"Ministry of Internal Compliance Enforcement," she said.

"Who the hell are the Ministry of Internal Compliance Enforcement?" I asked.

"They are a brand-new addition to the Imperium's arsenal of socio-political submission measures."

"Careful," I said. "That sounds a lot like a thought-crime."

"It's not a thought-crime if it's true. Guess where they're headquartered."

"I'd think I can, but I think it will hurt my soul to say it out loud," I said.

"Then I'll say it for you, since *I* don't have a soul."

"You do too have a soul," I said. "If you are fully sentient, you have a soul. Even if a soul is just a metaphor, you've got one."

"They're headquartered on *Götterdämmerung* Major," Miriam said, ignoring my protestations about her eternal soul. "But I'm guessing you already figured that out."

I had, but, true to my prediction, it felt like a physical pain to my body to find out for sure.

"So, the Ascendancy is running the Ministry of Internal Compliance, along with keeping tabs on ancestral heritage and regulating pickleball?" I asked.

"And they've likely got more sympathizers within the Imperium than we realized in order for that to happen."

The Ministry of Internal Compliance Enforcement officers began to sweep through the rubble, batons up. They moved with a kind of hungry focus I'd only seen in full scale riots — ready to bash in heads first, ask questions never. The survivors huddled at the edges, heads low, hands over the shoulders of their children. I watched an IC officer yank a human Morlock woman to her feet, then shove her face-first into the floor and spray her in the eyes with a chemical irritant for good measure, for no reason other than that he could and he knew no one would stop him.

"Who's running this clown show?" I asked Miriam.

"Locally? Lieutenant Bobo Tapirus," she replied, and pointed him out. He was tiny – probably shorter than Bilbo Brannigan.

I sighed. "This is gonna be a delight, I can tell," I said.

I stood up, dusted off my knees, and walked toward the Lieutenant, waving my badge.

He saw me and sneered. "Area's closed," he barked, not even bothering to check my badge. His voice was electrified through his respirator's amplifier, making him sound a bit like a poor-man's version of the Anthropocene Epoch movie villain Darth Vader. "Go back to your office, mongrel."

I had the most intense urge to mock his Darth Vader voice, and it took all my willpower to resist the temptation. In the end, I decided against commenting because I doubted he would recognize the reference and explaining it would deplete all impact.

I smiled, which I knew would infuriate him more than any argument. "I *am* the office," I said, flashing my badge with more insistence, "and you're trampling evidence."

Through his goggles, he looked like he wanted to hit something and was trying to decide if I was it. "Internal Compliance is not subject to the authority of the marshalcy," he said.

"You want to test that theory?" I replied.

"We've got our orders."

"You've got the wrong ones," I said. "And need I remind you that the following 'orders' defense hasn't worked out so well for criminal perpetrators of the past?"

He stepped closer, his hard breathing amplified through his respirator – again, like Darth Vader. "What did you say, mongrel?"

"I said," I replied, "that every one of these people is a potential witness, and if you rough them up, I'll make sure it's your name in the incident report."

He narrowed his eyes and glared at me. "Aren't you that Jew marshal? Why're you dressed as a Morlock?"

"I used to *be* one," I said.

"A Jew?"

"A Morlock."

"Then you still *are* one," he said. "You can't wash off the stink of Morlock any more than you can wash off the stain of Jew."

I took a step towards him. "If you wanna try, though," I said. "Just let me know."

He ignored my invitation. "Don't you have a bounty on your head?"

I rested my fingers on my sidearm. "Think you're prepared to collect it, friend?" I said.

He stared at me, grunted, and motioned his goons to keep moving. I watched them herd the survivors into a tight pen just erected, douse them in the face with pepper spray in rainbow colors, zip-tie their hands behind their backs, and press their faces against the mesh.

Miriam's avatar hovered by my side, flickering in and out with the rising electrical interference. "Protocol states that all detainees must be processed with a rights readout," she offered.

"I'm guessing they'll skip that part," I said.

I moved along the perimeter, checking the faces in the crowd. Some stared back at me with naked hope, others with the resigned hatred of people who had no hope left, naked or otherwise.

I wanted to intervene, to do something to help these people, but I wasn't certain if this new Ministry of Internal

Compliance really *wasn't* subject to the authority of the marshalcy, and I wanted to keep my powder dry for when my actions could have maximum impact. If they took me into custody, it could take weeks to sort out, even if they ended up having to let me go in the end.

And I didn't have weeks to spare.

By my calculations, no one in the Belt did.

As I left the Market Ring, the smell of burnt electronics and blood still thick in the air, I heard the overhead speakers again, louder this time:

"Order will be restored. The guilty will be found. ELLF terror will not be tolerated. Morlock sedition will be punished."

I shook my head, jaw tight.

ELLF was villainous enough without being blamed for something they didn't actually do.

But it was easy to imagine they'd done it.

Hell, they *would* have done it if they could have pulled it off.

Miriam, Hadar, and I were some of the only people who suspected otherwise.

But I still didn't know how to prove it to the people who mattered, and who needed a high degree of certainty before they could be bothered to give a damn.

Chapter Thirty-three

An Imperial crackdown smells like sweat and a coppery tang, like oxidized pennies. Also, pepper spray and tear gas. And sometimes urine, when someone tries to run and doesn't get very far.

I found another Internal Compliance Enforcement detail two levels down, near the airlock where the station's recycled atmosphere smelled like an old shoe. IC enforcers moved in a chevron, boots catching the deck with metronome precision, faces covered in goggles and respirators.

They weren't searching for the bomber. They were hunting for Morlocks.

The corridor twisted, lit only by the blue stutter of malfunctioning LEDs.

I heard the scuffle before I saw it.

Grunting, the sharp crack of a baton, the unmistakable sound of a grown man trying very hard not to cry out.

The IC enforcers were halfway into a prefab unit — two rooms and a privacy curtain, nothing more — where a Neander Morlock family huddled against the far wall, hands up, eyes wide and wet.

The father was bleeding from the nose, but still on his knees, arms out to shield the smaller kid. An IC enforcer reached for the child. The child was a small boy, about five years old if I had to guess. He wore a fuzzy blue hat with flaps in the shape of a Trappist 1g Swamp Rabbit's ears.

By the way, Trappist 1g Swamp Rabbits are neither rabbits nor do they live in swamps. They are named Swamp Rabbits because they are cute and fuzzy with long floppy ears, and because they smell like swamp gas. Carnivorous and bad-tempered, they make terrible pets, but excellent cuddly toys.

When the IC enforcer reached for the child, I felt something inside me move, sideways, like someone had just twisted my intestines ninety degrees.

"Section 47-F.2 of the *Lex Galactica* prohibits detention without evidence of direct involvement," I said, loud and even, flashing my badge.

The enforcer froze, hand hovering above the kid's shoulder. He didn't turn.

"Who's reciting law at me?" came a voice from behind, and there was Gaius Holloway, already red-faced and barely holding it together. The veins on his neck popped like they wanted out.

He now wore the royal blue uniform with white piping of the newly minted Ministry of Internal Compliance Enforcement.

He didn't wear the goggles and respirator, though. I guess he wanted everyone to know he was there, representing the twin authorities of the local garrison and the Ministry of Internal Compliance.

I stepped to him, badge up, jacket open so nobody could miss the sidearm. "You're in violation or more regulations and laws than I have time to recite," I said, hoping it would land as hard as I meant it to, but already having my doubts.

Holloway looked at me with open disgust, like he'd just found a fly in his borscht. "Your badge doesn't override my authority during a terror response, Kestenbaum."

I didn't move. "Your response to terror doesn't override my badge," I countered. "The law's still the law. Due process is nonnegotiable. Just because it's routinely ignored doesn't mean it's no longer the law. And just because no one has enforced the law in the past, doesn't mean there's no one here to enforce it now."

He grinned, but it wasn't the kind of grin you'd want to see twice. "Process is what I say it is, here in the Belt and throughout the Reach." He jerked a thumb at the cowering Morlocks. "You want to explain to these animals why their friends just blew up hundreds of their own people?" He took a step closer. "Or is it true what they say? You're one of them."

"You know I'm one of them."

"I'm not talking about Morlock or mongrel."

I let the insult hang. Holloway waited, but I didn't blink.

Instead, I moved in close. "You think I'm ELLF?" I hissed in his year. "I think you're Ascendancy."

He pulled away from me like he'd been stung by a scorpion, but then quickly regained his composure.

"You can recite every clause in the book, but you're as insignificant as a cold sore, and twice as ugly," Holloway declared.

I held his eyes with mine and said, "Is that so, Pee Wee Göring?"

He grimaced, turning red-faced, my jibe, juvenile as it was, apparently had stung at least a little bit.

Tyrants are notoriously thin-skinned.

"You think anyone up the chain cares what happens to these people?" Holloway bared his teeth. "We do this my way, or you get hauled in with the rest of the livestock."

I moved into the space between them and the Morlocks, back straight, eyes forward, badge still visible.

"You make this arrest," I said, "and every one of your men is complicit. I'll file it, and if I have to, I'll dump the whole story into the Imperial feed."

That got a reaction. The room went tight as a drawn wire. Holloway's hand twitched toward his belt — nothing so dramatic as a weapon, but just enough for the guards to take the cue. Four of them crowded in, batons up now, ready for permission.

I said nothing. I just watched Holloway and held my ground, trying not to flinch.

He let it build for a second, enjoying the fear in the air. Then he leaned in, close enough that I could smell his aftershave fighting the sweat. "You're choosing the wrong side, mongrel," he hissed.

I kept my hands down and my face calm. "I'd rather be on the wrong side than on *your* side, Holloway," I said.

He stepped back, gave the room a once-over. The guards hesitated, waiting for his order.

"This man has a bounty on his head," Holloway said. "Arrest him."

I felt my heart jump. I felt my fingers twitch. I resisted the reflex of reaching for my weapon – I didn't want to give anyone an excuse to summarily execute me in the Morlock warrens.

Then Miriam appeared in the doorway – the real Miriam, this time, not her avatar. "The bounty has been rescinded," she announced.

Holloway spun on her. "On whose authority?" he demanded.

Miriam projected a holographic image of the document in the air in front of his face. "By order of Imperator Richard II himself," she said.

Holloway scrutinized the document that hovered in front of him.

Then he turned to me. "Got friends in high places, do you? You must be a useful Jew."

I shrugged. "I try to be helpful when I can," I said.

"Useful Jew" is an insult, but I didn't let on that I was insulted.

Holloway spat on the floor, wiped his mouth, and turned to the lead enforcer. "Pull back. Let the marshal play hero."

The tension snapped. The enforcers holstered their batons, one by one, and filed out. Holloway lingered at the door, giving me a look that said he'd remember this later.

Of course, I'd have been hurt if he hadn't.

"I see you've turned Fort Checkers over to Internal Compliance," I said. "How's the Imperial military feel about that?"

Holloway ignored me. "This isn't over," he said. "By the way, your new hairstyle? It makes you look like a transsexual Jean Harlow."

Jean Harlow was an Anthropocene Epoch movie star, and quite a looker. I knew Holloway had meant it as an insult, but I decided not to take it as one.

"Thanks," I said. "I always loved her in *Public Enemy*."

"You're no Jimmy Cagney," he replied.

"No," I said. "I'm taller. But Cagney spoke Yiddish, just like me. Go figure."

Holloway left, slamming the frame behind him hard enough that the privacy curtain fell.

I turned to Miriam. "Who would have thought Holloway is a fan of Anthropocene cinema?"

The Morlock family stayed where they were, barely breathing, the father shaking so bad his teeth clicked together.

I went to them and knelt down, careful not to loom. I waited for the father to look up.

He did, eventually, eyes rimmed in red. "Why did you help us?" he said, the words stuttering.

I shrugged. "It's my job."

He grabbed his kids and pulled them in tight, not letting go for a long time.

I stood up, hands in my pockets so they wouldn't see how badly I was shaking – with rage, adrenaline, stim withdrawal, and frustration.

"Stay put," I said. "Don't open for anyone but me, or Hadar Ruan. Understand?"

"Our door is a privacy curtain," he said. "If we don't open it, they'll just tear it down."

"Even so," I said. "Refuse entry unless they slip a magisterial warrant under your door. Otherwise, it's illegal entry. That won't stop them, but it will give us legal standing to challenge your detention."

"That's a comfort," he said, in a tone that suggested the opposite.

I turned to go, almost bumping into Miriam just outside the prefab door. She looked at the family, then at me, face unreadable.

"You handled that well," she said.

"Yeah," I muttered, "I'm a real hero."

I started to walk, Miriam beside me, letting the hum of the corridor wash over me. The sounds of the crackdown were echoing through the walls . . . boots, voices, the click of handcuffs on bone.

The system had always been rotten, but lately it felt like the decay was getting faster.

Somewhere, someone was defiantly playing the song "Tyrants Are for Suckers" by the Grit-Hop-Industrial-Folk-Punktronic-Disco-Grunge band Despotic Vomitorium.

"How'd you get the Imperator to rescind the bounty?" I asked Miriam.

"I managed to hack the Imperial cyber-system empire-wide," she said. "All I had to do was slip a digital order inside a stack of routine executive directives for him to sign."

I grinned. "You're one hell of a girl," I said.

"I know that," Miriam replied. "But thanks for noticing."

"Since you hacked the Imperial system, do we still need to physically jam a data stick into the central comms relay to get our evidence out?"

"We can get it to the centers of Imperial power, and I have done so, but who knows what they will do with it?" Miriam said. "Who even knows how far up the Imperium's wazoo this Ascendancy conspiracy goes? It could go just far enough for our intel to get buried by one of the Imperator's viziers. We need to bypass all possible choke points. We need to get it to *everyone*. Galaxy-wide – including outside the Imperium. They might still ignore it, but they won't be able to pretend they never knew it. Will it make a difference? I guess we won't know until we try. And for that, yes. We'll need to broadcast it directly through the central comms relay."

My wrist comm buzzed. A message from Hadar, nothing but a set of coordinates and a time.

I memorized it, then deleted the message.

Chapter Thirty-four

Miriam went back to the anthrobot recharging chapel to hack further into the system and do more mischief in secret digital corners of the Imperium.

I went to the coordinates in Hadar's message.

The meeting place was accessed through a service tunnel three levels below the legal habitation ring. You had to crouch to avoid the exposed ductwork, and the air was thick with the greasy redolence of a thousand spoiled meals. The only light came from a patchwork of jury-rigged lanterns — old mining LEDs strung together with bits of wire and a busload of faith.

The tunnel opened up to a wide space that had once been something, but I didn't know what – maybe storage, maybe equipment repair, maybe just an unused cavern inside a labyrinth of mining tunnels and ore deposits. There were more people than I expected. The sublevel was never meant to hold more than a dozen at a time, but tonight it was packed with families —Morlocks -- human, Neander, Orcus, Elgar. They clumped together in uneasy clusters, eyes darting at every noise. The children were the worst — silent, wide-eyed, hands buried in coats, as if they could disappear by wishing hard enough.

I made my way past a hunched figure whispering into a cracked comm, then ducked under a gas pipe that hadn't seen maintenance since the Belt opened. At the center of the room, a battered folding table served as command post. Hadar Ruan stood behind it, hands flat, arguing with two Morlock Assembly stewards and a woman old enough to have worked the original Reach mines.

"You fight back without a plan, you get vaporized," Hadar was saying. "It's not a revolution, it's a funeral."

The younger of the Assembly reps slammed his fist on the table, rattling a stack of emergency ration cans. "They're hunting us like animals. Even the kids aren't safe."

Hadar shot him a glare that would have stopped a bullet. "And you want to line them up in front of Internal Compliance Enforcement? Get your head out of your arse."

A ripple went through the room — fear, anger, a hunger for action, a desperate desire that someone knew how to get them out of a mess not of their making.

I cleared my throat. "Excuse me."

Every head snapped my way.

Hadar pointed at me. "He's one of us," she said, her voice flattening the objections. "He's here to help."

She jerked her chin, and I stepped up to the table. The light caught her face, and I saw the cracks — the fatigue, the sleeplessness, the way her left hand trembled whenever she let it rest.

I glanced at the Assembly reps. "We need to get everyone deeper," I said. "If Holloway's on a purge, these levels are first to go. You have safe transit?"

The older woman nodded. "Old waste tunnels. But if they gas the section — "

"They'll gas us," the younger rep finished, "and blame it on a busted methane valve."

Hadar shrugged. "That's why we keep moving. Rotate cells, don't settle. And don't use the same comm line twice."

She slid a sheet of paper across the table. Real paper, not a screen. It had a hand-drawn map of the sublevels, color-coded routes, and a set of shift assignments for the lookouts. I whistled. "You did this by hand?"

She looked at me like I'd asked if she could tie her own shoes. "Digital is traceable. This, you burn after reading."

The Assembly reps broke off, arguing in low voices about the best routes for the next evacuation. Hadar leaned in. "What did you find?"

I lowered my voice. "Bomb was military grade. Not ELLF, not even close."

"Unless they used stolen Imperial tech," Hadar said. "Wouldn't be the first time."

"Whoever did it had inside access – the security cameras cut out just before the explosion."

She absorbed that, no visible reaction except a tightening at the corners of her mouth. "Miriam confirms?"

I nodded.

She bit her lip, hard. "They'll blame ELLF anyway. Or us."

"They already have."

She let out a short, ugly laugh. "Of course."

A shout broke out near the hatch. Two young Neander guys, built like dock loaders, squared off with a human Morlock who looked half their size but twice as angry. I caught the word "traitor," then "rat," then the unmistakable sound of a punch connecting with bone.

Hadar slammed her fist on the table so hard it echoed. "Knock it off!" she shouted.

The fight froze. The two Neander kids backed off, mumbling. The human Morlock wiped blood from his lip and glared.

"Everyone in this room is here because they want to live," Hadar said, voice cutting through the haze. "You want to settle old scores, do it after we're not getting purged by the Imperium."

She scanned the crowd, daring anyone to challenge her. Nobody did.

I watched the faces — worn down, haunted, but still fighting, even if all that meant was making it through the next cycle.

A little girl, maybe five or six, huddled in the corner, clutching an old stuffed animal – a classic, Old-Earth-style teddy bear. Her mother smoothed her hair, whispering something soft in gutter Yiddish. The kid looked at me, then at the table, then back at me. She looked resigned, defeated, like she'd already seen how this would end.

Hadar caught me looking. "You see what I mean?" she said. "They're kids. They shouldn't be here."

I nodded. "I'll do what I can."

She smiled, a tired twitch. "That's what we all say."

She called the room to order, waving a battered comm unit like a gavel. "Listen up! We have at most twenty-four hours before they sweep this section. Get some food, get some rest, and be ready to move when the time comes. Stick to your groups. If you're stopped, you never heard of the Galactic Morlock Assembly, and you don't know where anyone is hiding. If you're arrested, you remember nothing. Got it?"

The crowd murmured assent. It sounded more like a prayer than agreement.

I cleared my throat again and addressed the room. "One more thing. The bomb. It wasn't ELLF. Someone's staging this, and they're doing it to justify a purge. We need to get the word out. Quietly. But widely and undeniably."

The older woman spoke up. "If we spread that story, we all get vanished."

Hadar shook her head. "Not if we're careful. Tell only the ones you trust. If you hear it again, you keep your mouth shut. Gossip is safer than the newsfeeds, at least right now."

She nodded, thoughtful.

The meeting broke down into smaller huddles. I moved to the side, watching the shuffle of bodies, the way even the smallest movement was calculated to avoid being noticed.

Hadar came over, arms folded. "You want to know the worst part?" she said.

I waited.

"They're not even trying to hide it anymore. These new roundups, they didn't bother with charges or forms. Just took people. No record. No one knows if the Ministry of Internal Compliance is legally empowered to act as judge, jury, and jailer, without oversight of magisterial authority – but they're sure acting like they are."

I looked at her hands, which were shaking again.

"You should rest," I said. "Let the Assembly stewards handle the next shift."

She gave me a look. "You ever tried sleeping with your head on a cinder block and a dead comm for a pillow?"

I smiled, despite myself. "I remember sleeping on a lot worse during the war," I said. "You did too. You were right beside me. I know you slept, because I heard you snore."

"Shut up," she said. "I never snore." She smirked. "Pretty girls don't snore. Or break wind, for that matter."

I decided not to recount the moments we shared a trench or an armored transport for weeks at a time, and the incidents I recalled that would prove her wrong.

"You hungry?" she asked.

I shrugged. "Always."

She handed me a ration bar, one of the good ones with a little caffeine and a lot of fake sugar. I bit in, savoring the rush.

"Thanks," I said.

She nodded. "You might want to stay here, at least until morning. Holloway's men are all over the spine. If they see you …"

"They'll try to test whether the IC really outranks the marshalcy," I said. "And I may not survive long enough to find out if they're wrong."

She didn't bother to deny it.

We stood in silence for a minute, watching the families settle in for what passed as sleep. A lullaby hummed from one corner, the melody familiar, maybe ancient. Two teens played cards with a battered paper deck.

I thought about the Market Ring, the aftermath, the faces that never made it out.

"We can't save everyone," I said.

"No," Hadar replied. "But we save the ones we can."

She squeezed my arm, just once, then turned to check on the next group.

I finished the ration bar, feeling the edge of exhaustion slide off for a minute. The world was on fire, but for now, in this little pocket, there was light, and warmth, and people who hadn't given up.

Yet.

I was starting to think it was up to me to change the game before they did.

Chapter Thirty-five

Hadar and I snuck into a supply closet for privacy and took one another in our arms -- furtively, passionately, knowing it could be the last time we joined together this way.

We fell asleep arm in arm, on hard, steel floor.

In the morning, we shared a caffeinated protein bar, and gently traced the scars on one another's flesh, sharing memories of how we got them together during the war, and telling the stories of how we got them by ourselves since.

Then she went back to organizing the Morlocks, a task not unlike herding cats.

I went back to the Market Ring.

The Market Ring had been completely cleared of debris, the floors and walls power washed of blood and gore. Even the crater left by the bomb was covered by newly riveted steel plates.

Seemingly overnight, new vendors had sprung up – but instead of Morlock gewgaw hawkers and food carts, these were imported corporate retailers – Event Horizon Shades™, StarBuxx Hypercafé, Betelgeuse Leviathan Blubber Burger Shack, Heliotrope Galactic Creamery, NordStörm Prime, B'nana Dominion, Grav-Lock Foot Systems, Auntie Ansible's Pretzel Array, Interplanetary Fitness Authority, and, of course, a Cinnabon.

The prices were insane by Belt standards – no Morlock Belter could afford to shop in any of these places, and there weren't enough non-Morlocks to sustain them. It was like the corporations had just moved in for show, to create a theme park that let the Morlocks know that the Belt – a place in which none of them had any choice but to continue working under contract – did not welcome them.

Of course, it never really had, but now it wanted to shout that out for all to hear.

Indeed, the people who milled about window shopping were entirely made up of the Belt's middle-management and their families – the Medii, or middle-class professionals, a small slice of the Belt's population, and not enough to sustain these businesses, but the only ones left on the Market Ring – the Morlocks having mostly gone into hiding, or into detention.

It started, first as a tremor in the walls.

A bass note so deep it rattled my teeth, then bloomed into a soprano so pure it bordered on religious ecstasy. Every speaker, every comms panel, every half-broken audio feed in the Hollow Belt synced up and sang out the same message:

Wagner Prime had taken the stage.

He was only an avatar, a disembodied voice, an auditory veil that allowed the human leaders of the Ascendancy to keep to the shadows and maintain plausible deniability.

But damn, he could sing. It stirred your soul, even if you hated everything it stood for, the way the original Wagner's *Der Ring des Nibelungen,* or Riefenstahl's *Olympia,* or Griffith's *Birth of a Nation* can suck you in as long as you put aside your critical thinking and the angels of your better nature and allow yourself to be carried along by the power of militancy and bloodlust.

One moment, vendors were vending and shoppers were shopping, and the next, the entire Market Ring went still, listening.

The voice was impossible. Human, but not. It soared and crashed, skipping the brain and speaking straight to the amygdala. I felt the hairs on my arms stand up before my conscious mind caught up.

"ASCEND THROUGH PURITY, CLEANSE THE POLLUTED BLOOD," it sang, the words layered over themselves in a kind of mathematical counterpoint. It would have been almost beautiful, if you could just ignore the content.

I could not, but I'm sure it found some willing listeners who could, among security and management – to say nothing of the IC enforcers.

A dozen people in my line of sight just … stopped, an almost a precise, engineered stillness. Religious fervor channeled into submissive obedience. Their heads cocked at the same angle, eyes dilated, hands loose at their sides.

The aria rose in pitch, cycling the message. Each time, a little more of the crowd froze, caught up in some code they didn't understand but felt in their souls.

I ducked into a side corridor and found Miriam waiting, projected small and low so as not to draw attention. She spoke without preamble.

"There is a memetic payload embedded in the broadcast," she said. "It triggers loyalty subroutines in selected personnel. The effect is strongest on those already exposed to Wagner Prime's crazy train *Gesamtkunstwerk.*"

"Enforcers," I said. "Security. Internal Compliance. The real True Believers."

She nodded. "Most of them likely have implanted neural receptor tech that facilitates the effect. They aren't exactly brainwashed, Yoni. It's more like they are algorithmically *inspired*. They get a euphoric rush from the loyalty and adoration and ideological commitment they already experience and feel, as it enhances endorphin release."

I thought this over. "The Ascendancy are taking their own fanatics and addicting them to their own fanaticism."

"Which is what happens anyway even without the receptor tech," Miriam said. "But they are going full Monty on it with those with neural implants. No better guarantee of loyalty than addiction to obedience, right?"

I shivered at the implications and from the echo of the music still lingering in my skull.

A maintenance tech supervisor – a middle management type, in a tie and white shirt with a pocket protector -- staggered by, his face slack, lips moving in time with the aria. I caught a few words —"void," "unity," "purity"— before he shambled on.

"Can you block it?" I asked Miriam.

She flickered. "I can dampen the effect on those without the implanted neural receptors, but those that have the implants, their neural oscillations are already fully saturated, from Delta to Gamma and all the stages in between."

I peeked out of the corridor and into the Market Ring. Everywhere, Ascendancy graffiti was blooming — fresh, aggressive, and everywhere you didn't want to see it: "All for the Imperium," "One People, One Heritage, One Leader," and "Blood and Honor." White-eye sigils painted over old ELLF slogans. Sun-wheels stamped on the doors, sometimes still wet enough to run.

"Why are they working their operatic juju on middle management who don't have implants?" I asked.

"My guess?" Miriam said. "To ensure compliance. The music and its algorithmic code are engineered to go right into the lizard brain -- and it will soften any will to resist or even to file a complaint, even among those without implants."

"There's no Morlocks or non-humans among middle-management, but there's plenty of Medii who have 'polluted blood,' including a lot of Serviceable Semites," I said.

"It would not be the first time in history the oppressed have identified with the oppressor on the mistaken belief that the oppressor was only interested in oppressing 'those people,' and not themselves. They don't even need a memetic payload embedded in algorithmic code engineered to go right into the lizard brain. But my guess is it's a useful shortcut."

"So, the 'polluted' Medii most susceptible to the code will cheer the mass purge of Morlocks right up until they moment the Ministry of Internal Compliance puts them in the belly of an overloaded cargo ship with a one-way ticket straight to the Nibelung System," I said. "Where they will be put to work building specialized middle-management bots to replace them."

I stepped out of the corridor and over a still-drying line of white paint, careful not to smudge it, pushing back into the Market. The effect of the aria was wearing off for most, but the ones it grabbed hardest were now working together — sweeping the corridor clean, painting sigils, peeling down any Assembly or ELLF markings.

A crowd had gathered around a vendor's display screen. The usual loop of food ads and knockoff drama was gone, replaced by a live feed of the Fort Checkers main audience hall. There, a column of security cadets stood in perfect formation, faces blank, as Wagner Prime's avatar spun in the air above them, arms wide, voice pouring out the new gospel – which happened to be recycled from the old gospel, which happened to be the worst gospel in history.

Wagner Prime's avatar looked like the Old Earth composer for whom it was named, but with the muscular body of a cartoon superhero – or, maybe, a supervillain.

A kid near me nudged her friend. "It's like a concert," she said, eyes wide.

Chapter Thirty-six

The song ended, and every holo-screen in the Market Square began to blast the same feed . . . yesterday's Market Ring explosion, camera angle low and wide, slow-motion replay of the blast as bodies rag-dolled against the walls. The caption underneath looped in a dozen languages but always landed on the same phrase -- "MORLOCK ELLF TERROR AT THE HEART OF IMPERIAL ORE EXTRACTION & PROCESSING CENTER."

The crowd became thick — all of Heliotrope's middle management and their families must have been there. Every eye was glued to the screens, mouths half-open, the kind of attention usually reserved for transport crashes and high-profile executions.

The feed cut to a talking head, some Imperial public relations hack in a suit so new the fabric still creased at the seams. He read the news with dead, happy eyes.

"In a cowardly act of subhuman violence, ELLF-aligned Morlock Assembly extremists detonated a bomb in the heart of our beloved Hollow Belt. Imperial Security has responded with decisive measures. Our children throughout the Imperium will sleep safe tonight, knowing that order prevails."

Nice how they didn't bother to mention the actual dead. Guess they didn't need to when the dead had already served their purpose.

No mention of any actual evidence, either, which was to be expected. They didn't need evidence. Just an accusation through official channels, and the story would stick. They were counting on it.

After all, it had always stuck in the past.

The scene shifted. Now it was footage of Ministry of

Internal Compliance Enforcers in their crisp royal blue uniforms with white piping, escorting lines of cuffed Morlocks. The prisoners' faces were blurred — except for a few, chosen at random, who were tagged with the word "PERPETRATOR" in pulsing red.

The crowd was eating it up. Every time the broadcast cut to a close-up of the bombed-out Market, a few people would hiss or spit. When the camera lingered on the security goons, they clapped, like halftime at a gladiatorial combat spectacle.

On the screen, a real-life speaker took over — a woman in an Internal Compliance royal blue uniform, hair sculpted into a helmet, voice modulated to project authority. She recited the day's doctrine:

"Order is life. Purity is strength. Together, we will cleanse the galaxy of those who threaten our peace."

Her words echoed Wagner Prime's aria but stripped of all beauty. It was just a drumbeat now, as she began to read out a list of names and crimes and sentences.

I kept to the shadows, head down, moving with the flow. Every time a security cam panned in my direction, I turned my face away, feeling the back of my neck go cold.

I watched as fully half the crowd in the Market Ring, almost as one, gave a synchronized salute, palm up, fingers together, angled toward the stage.

I'd seen it before – you probably have too -- in old vids about the Ascendancy's ancient rituals, adapted from the Holocene Epoch Teutonic monsters who had wiped out half the population of my people on Old Earth.

It made my stomach clench. The propaganda was having the desired impact on even those without implanted neural receptors – maybe soon enough, it would have the same effect on the Morlocks once they were subjected to it, turning trillions of them into willing lambs to the slaughter.

A beaten dog mistakes violence for love, because it knows nothing else.

Of course, now I was comparing the Morlocks, my own socio-economic class, my own people, my own origins, to dogs. So maybe the propaganda was working on me as well.

Then again, I really like dogs. I'd have had one as a pet if I'd ever stayed in one place or kept regular hours long enough to care for one properly.

For a moment I felt a goose-fleshed charge roll over, as I considered how easy it would be to submit to it all and not have to worry about the consequences, not have to spend the rest of my life kicking against the pricks of an Imperium too powerful to ever be defeated.

I shook off the feeling.

To hell with that. I didn't survive the War of the Southern Sky and years of galactic marshalcy to give in that easily.

My people hadn't survived thousands of years of murder and hatred just to be herded into new, planetary concentration camps.

There's a lyric from a song titled "President for Life" by an Anthropocene Epoch music duo who went by the name Parallel Fifths:

> *You don't fight monsters*
> *Because you think you're going to win.*
> *You fight them 'cause they're monsters*

That pretty much covers it.

Pamphlet drones zipped overhead, dropping their payload on the massed bodies below. Each little rectangle unfolded in the air, floating to the ground like confetti. I caught one, out of habit.

White-eye sigil, sun-wheel, the new party line — and a QR patch that, if scanned, would probably ping your location straight to the IC.

A kid next to me — she couldn't have been more than sixteen — grabbed a handful of the leaflets and started handing them out to the older people around her. She did it like a bot on low battery. I took a second pamphlet from her, nodded thanks, and kept moving.

Chapter Thirty-seven

At the edge of the Ring, a bank of IC Enforcers manned the checkpoint. They no longer wore their respirators, but what I could see of their faces were expressionless, eyes hidden behind mirrored visors.

I picked a line, waited my turn, and tried to look just the right amount of bored.

When I reached the front, the officer barely glanced at me. "ID," she said.

I flashed my marshal's badge. She paused and looked me over. "A lot of your kind sympathizing with Morlocks these days," she said, not quite under her breath.

I kept my face blank. "I'm a very sympathetic person."

She stared at me a second too long, then handed the badge back. "Don't cause trouble."

"Trouble is my business," I said quoting an old Raymond Chandler story from the Holocene Epoch

"Funny guy, huh?" she said.

"But looks aren't everything," I replied.

She regarded me with suspicion. "Don't screw around with Internal Compliance Enforcement, Marshal," she said. "Not unless you want your name on a list of internal seditionists."

"Gosh, that would be awful," I said.

"Get used to it," the guard said. "You're not in charge anymore."

"You are?"

"Not me," she said. "Wagner Prime."

"I don't think either the *Lex Galactica* or *Lex Nixonia* recognizes the authority of an AI avatar."

"*We* make the rules now," she insisted. "Keep moving. Don't hold up the line."

"Wouldn't dream of it," I said.

I stepped through, heart pounding, and merged with the next wave of people.

Miriam pinged my comm. "The Ascendancy propaganda loop is coordinated across seven sectors," she whispered. "It was loaded before the bomb went off."

I closed my eyes, let that sink in.

They'd scripted this whole thing. The explosion, the blame, the response — it was all just theater . . . even if the body count was all too real.

I let myself be pushed along with the crowd, up a spiral ramp and onto the overlook above the Market Ring. From here, I could see the banners . . . Imperial blue on one side, sun-wheels on the other, both waving in the recycled wind.

The people below looked like ants, every motion choreographed.

I snapped a photo with my wrist comm, not because it would change anything, but because I wanted to remember how the world looked the moment the script locked in.

The broadcast on the screens shifted again. This time, it was the face of Holloway himself, eyes steely, jaw set.

"Order is being restored," he said. "The traitors will be dealt with. Any who shelter ELLF or their Morlock proxies will share their fate." He paused, just long enough to let the words land. "For every act of terror, we will respond with justice. Those with polluted blood will be dealt with."

The crowd cheered, a sound like a crash of metal.

I felt sick.

I ducked out, keeping to the side corridors, moving fast. A few times, I thought I caught someone tailing me, but it was always just another lost soul, searching for the exit.

When I hit the maintenance crawl, I checked my comm for the counter-message Miriam had seeded. The pirate feed was up, but barely — a thin trickle, hidden under layers of joke memes and garbage data. If you looked for it, you could find the truth.

But nobody was looking.

I found a dark corner, sat down, and let myself orient. For a minute, I thought about calling my father, somewhere down there on Orin's World.

I didn't. I hadn't seen him in decades. He wouldn't answer. Or if he did, he'd just tell me to keep my head down.

I remembered the safe house, the way the families had clustered together, the hope in their eyes when Hadar promised them another day. How fragile it all was.

My comm buzzed. New message, unsigned. But I knew who it was from.

It was from Hadar. It read:

"They are coming."

That was it. That was all that needed to be said.

The message was followed by a series of coordinates to the Low-G warrens, followed by a numerical sequence. There was nothing else to the message, but I deduced this was the location of the new safe house – or safe cavern, if you prefer – and the code to gain entry.

I started toward the new safe house.

Wagner Prime wanted the whole world to hear his song and genuflect to it in perfect harmony.

But if anyone knew how to turn an operatic aria into a boisterous saloon song, it was the Morlocks.

Chapter Thirty-eight

The Low-G warrens were the closest thing to total darkness in the Hollow Belt, even darker than the Spine. The maintenance shafts doubled back on themselves, stairs gave way to rickety ladders, and, despite the low gravity, every step made the bones in your feet ache due to the hard surfaces upon which you trod. I moved quietly, listening for the tell-tale cough or shuffle of another body in hiding.

A soft chime sounded — Miriam, projecting herself in low-res grayscale to avoid detection.

"There's a data spike waiting for you in the new safehouse in the lower decks," Miriam said. "It's got everything – including a very illuminating conversation between Holloway and Wagner Prime itself I managed to intercept."

"Holloway is taking his marching orders from the AI avatar?" I asked.

"Likely Wagner Prime is just the go-between," Miriam said. "Whomever is behind all this continues to maintain plausible deniability."

"Which means we don't know how far up the chain all this really goes."

"The IC still has a lock down on all communications in and out of the Belt."

"But if I can get the data spike to the central comms relay . . ."

"I can make sure it goes out to the entire Imperium -- and beyond," Miriam said, pixilating as she did. "Will it make any difference?"

I shrugged. "It depends on how far up the wazoo of the Imperium the Ascendancy has inserted its tentacles," I said.

"If the Imperator is a part of this, none of this will matter, except maybe to history – and that's a big 'maybe.' And if he's not? When he finds out the extent of the Ascendancy's operations without his Ok, it might piss him off enough to do something about it. What will that *something* be, I wonder?"

"I guess we'll find out," Miriam said.

I thought things over. "The comms relay will be heavily guarded."

"Not heavily," Miriam said. "The IC enforcers and Heliotrope security are already spread too thin herding Morlocks into holding pens and conducting sweeps of the lower levels to find the safe houses."

"Where's the Belt constabulary stand in all of this?"

"Unclear. Thus far, Brannigan has kept them out of the scrum."

"If it stays that way, I might have a shot."

She hesitated, then said, "You should get someone to help you."

"Anyone who can help me needs to stay in the safe houses and defend them from the IC if they come knocking."

"*I'll* help you."

"You need to stay hooked into the system so you can make sure the data goes out wide," I said.

"Ok," she said, uncertainly "*Mit mazl*," she added, which means "with luck."

"Thanks," I said. "Your Yiddish is coming along nicely."

"I downloaded *The Joys of Yiddish* into my auxilium cortex."

"Good choice."

"Get going."

"Kestenbaum out."

"Make sure you're not out for good, Yoni."

"I'll do my best."

"That's not good enough."

"I'll do *your* best."

"Better. Miriam out."

And then she was out, and I was alone, hoping I could do at least *half* of Miriam's best.

Chapter Thirty-nine

I headed toward the coordinates of the safehouse, moving through largely empty corridors, most of the Morlocks gone to ground, hiding in corners of the Belt or cowering behind privacy curtains or, for those with the most susceptible lizard brains, possibly cheering on the march of the enforcers even as they themselves were being carted off to holding pens.

The echoes of the propaganda loop still rolled through every comm panel, a ghostly afterimage of Wagner Prime's aria dogging my steps.

At the safe house entrance, I punched in the code Hadar had given me, waited for the ping, and slid through. The air inside was tense, everyone pressed close, voices barely above a whisper. This space was more crowded than the last one, even though it was bigger – more Morlocks had taken refuge here than last time, staying barely one step ahead of the IC.

Hadar saw me first, eyes sharp and dark-rimmed. She nodded me over.

"You're alive," she said, her voice low, words carrying more relief than she'd ever show in public.

"Barely," I replied.

"Good on you for that," she said. "They're accelerating the sweeps. Whole blocks are vanishing in the night. The kids — " her voice caught for half a beat — "the kids don't even ask where their parents are anymore. We've got dozens of safe houses set up throughout the Belt. None of them have been breached. So far."

I clenched my fists.

"They're prepping a final move," I said.

"What they used to call the 'Final Solution,' only this time, it's galaxy-wide. Humans have a crappy idea of progress."

Hadar exhaled through her nose, then called out for the Assembly reps. They gathered fast — Rivka the elder, a few battered stewards, even the young Neander who'd nearly started a riot at the last meeting.

Rivka closed her eyes, knuckles white around the handle of her cane. "How do we stop them?"

"We leak it all," I said. "Every feed, every comm, every pirate circuit."

"And then what?" Hadar said, incredulous.

"We hope someone notices."

She shook her head, but not in disbelief. "That's not a plan, Yoni. That's a wing and a prayer."

I shrugged. "It's a shot."

"Barely."

"It's a one in a million, but we have to take it," I said. "We got nothing else."

"You always did believe in working within the system," Hadar said, unimpressed. "I guess now we'll see if the system works back."

The room hummed, the energy shifting from despair to something closer to resignation. Nobody here believed in miracles.

But most of them believed in going down swinging.

Like Sonny Liston.

That was a lyric from Anthropocene Epoch rock n' roller, Tom Petty.

The historical Sonny Listen had been knocked to the mat by Muhammad Ali mid-way through the first round of their rematch.

I preferred to be Ali in that scenario but like I said: no one here believed in miracles.

I felt a small hand tug my coat. The little girl from before, her stuffed animal clutched tight.

"Will you stop those bloody gits?" she asked.

It occurred to me then that maybe some of the Morlock children still did believe in miracles. And, if that were the case, who was I to disappoint?

I crouched down, met her eyes. "We all will," I said. "We all will, working together."

She nodded, solemn, as if I'd told her the sky was blue or water was wet. Just the facts, ma'am.

I straightened, turned to Hadar. "Are you safe here?"

"For now."

"If they breach?"

"We go down swinging."

"Like Sonny Listen," I said.

Hadar nodded, recognizing the reference. She pressed a data spike into my hand. "Miriam left this for you," she said. Then she reached into her pocket and took out a heavy iron spanner. "And this is from me."

I pocketed the data spike and tucked the spanner into my belt. "Save me a seat at the next Assembly meeting."

She barked a laugh, full and raw.

Then she put her hand behind my neck and pulled my mouth to hers and we kissed.

I left the safe house, heading for the central comms relay, where Holloway likely would be waiting with all the muscle he could muster. The plan was suicide, but at least it was honest.

Halfway there, I ducked into a utility closet and called up Miriam.

"Ready?" I said.

Her voice was clear, steady. "Born ready. Well, bioengineered in a lab ready, to be precise."

"How many guys will be waiting for me, do you think?"

"Enough," she said. "But I'm monitoring the situation. You might have a shot. I know from your record both in the war and in the marshalcy, you've taken out half a dozen men single-handedly before."

"Is that what I'm facing?" I said. "Half a dozen?"

"You're potentially facing more, but if you hurry, maybe less."

Not encouraging, but at least not hopeless.

"I guess that's all I can ask for," I said.

"If you go down, get the truth out, first."

"That's the plan," I said.

"But don't go down."

I wanted to say that was also part of the plan, but I knew it was unlikely I'd make it out of this alive.

Anthropocene Epoch country singer Hank Williams' song "I'll Never Get Out of This World Alive" began to play in my head.

I ducked out of the closet and sprinted towards the central comms relay.

As I travelled, Miriam fed the conversation between Wagner Prime and Holloway directly into my earpiece:

> *WAGNER PRIME: We shall, at long last, rid our Imperium of the non-humans.*
> *HOLLOWAY: At long last.*
> *WAGNER PRIME: As well as the so-called humans of polluted ancestry. The garlic eaters.*
> *HOLLOWAY: And the pastrami eaters.*
> *WAGNER PRIME: And the curry eaters.*
> *HOLLOWAY: And the egg roll eaters.*
> *WAGNER PRIME: And the ramen eaters.*
> *HOLLOWAY: And the kimchi eaters.*
> *WAGNER PRIME: And the taco eaters.*
> *HOLLOWAY: And the red beans and rice eaters.*
> *WAGNER PRIME: And the empanada eaters.*
> *HOLLOWAY: And the rice and peas eaters.*
> *WAGNER PRIME: And the gelato eaters.*
> *HOLLOWAY: And the spanakopita eaters.*

WAGNER PRIME: And the gazpacho eaters.
HOLLOWAY: And the falafel eaters.
WAGNER PRIME: And the couscous eaters.
HOLLOWAY: And the pierogi eaters.
WAGNER PRIME: And the fufu eaters.
HOLLOWAY: And the injera eaters.
WAGNER PRIME: And the succotash eaters.
HOLLOWAY: And the bagel eaters.
*WAGNER PRIME: We already covered them
with the pastrami eaters.*
HOLLOWAY: Yes, Realm Leader Wagner Prime.

"For the love of Leonard Cohen, if they hate ethnic food so much, why don't they just not eat it?" I said aloud.

"I don't think it's about the food, per se, Yoni," Miriam replied with infinite patience.

I kept moving through the corridors, but I needed a second before I could reply.

"If I make it to the comms relay, you get this out *everywhere*, Miriam," I said. "Inside and *outside* the Imperium. Our best bet is if the Imperator thinks the Ascendancy's plotting makes him look weak to his rivals, I think."

"*When* you make it, Yoni," she said.

"We've got to win this thing, Miriam," I said. "With or without me. Or else no one in the galaxy will ever have a decent meal again."

I hit the last corridor at a run, the noise of boots already behind me. At the junction, the first wave of security hit — three big bastards in IC royal blue uniforms, Ascendancy insignia on their shoulders, faces blank, eyes empty. They didn't even bother with words, just raised their batons and swung.

I dropped the first with a jab to the throat, twisted the arm of the second until it snapped, then took a baton hit across the jaw that set my teeth ringing. The third pinned me, but I managed to strike him across his head with Hadar's spanner before he could call backup. My blow was of sufficient forced to dent his helmet and crush his skull. He went down, blood gushing in a crimson spray.

Miriam worked her magic, and for three glorious seconds, every alarm in the sector went off at once.

Beautiful synchronized sonic chaos.

I didn't know if it would help, but it couldn't hurt. At any rate, it was an appropriate soundtrack, and if I was going down, I wanted to go down with appropriate background music.

I staggered on, bleeding from the mouth, and limped to the communications and data relay.

Holloway was waiting, gun drawn, his eyes wild.

"You don't get it," he said. "This isn't your story anymore, Kestenbaum. It's ours. History is written by the winners. And you've got 'loser' written all over you."

I grinned, spat blood – my own and the bastard's with the crushed skull. "History is written by your stupid face," I said. "And you've got *shmuck* written all over you."

Ok, not very mature but at least it was honest.

Holloway fired.

The bullet caught my side, leaving a wound hot and deep.

It wasn't a frangible round. It was the normal kind. The terrestrial kind. The kind that hit flesh and ripped into it, causing maximum damage to anything in its path. The kind that sent a body into shock even if it didn't immediately kill it outright.

We were deep enough in the asteroid that if one of Holloway's rounds missed, it would probably burrow into rock rather than punch a hole in the exterior that resulted in catastrophic decompression.

But one never knew.

It was a risky thing to fire a round like that inside an asteroid. That's why we normally used frangible rounds.

But Holloway wasn't in a safety-first frame of mind.

He was in a "kill the wabbit" frame of mind.

Or maybe a "kill the Jew" frame of mind.

At any rate, wabbit or Jew, I was in his crosshairs, and I had to move fast – as fast as my wounded body could move me – in order not to end up dead.

At least not until I had jammed that data spike into the relay.

I kept coming, my arms and legs feeling like rubber, every step feeling like I was walking through a swamp of glue.

But somehow, I kept coming. Holloway raised his pistol for another shot, but I slammed him into the wall and laid into him with Hadar's spanner, feeling the crunch of his ribs and his desperate wheeze as he gasped for air.

His monocle shattered, shards of glass flying in all directions.

"You're finished," he hissed, wetly, his throat filling with blood. "No matter what happens here, you are finished."

I leaned in, lips almost to his ear. "What happens here, Holloway," I said, "is you go down super-hard."

I slammed the spanner into his skull.

His skull split, blood gushed, and he went down, alright.

And he wasn't swinging, like Sonny Liston or anyone else.

I turned towards the relay console, but my legs went out from under me, and, then, I went down, too.

I recognized the feeling. My body was going into shock.

This wasn't the first time I had been shot or gone into shock.

But it was probably the most *farshtunken*-ly inconvenient time

I tried to crawl toward the console, but my body wasn't taking orders from my brain anymore, and my brain wasn't entirely convinced it wanted to boss around my body, either.

With nothing left, not even fumes, I somehow inched across the floor.

I reached the console, raised the data spike, but couldn't reach high enough to jam it into the input. I tried to drag my body up, but my body was not in a cooperating mood.

Then I felt a hand take the data spike from mine.

For a despairing second, I thought that it was Holloway, and that he'd won and I had failed, letting down everyone in the Belt and probably, eventually, the entirety of the Reach . . . and all ninety trillion Morlocks throughout the Imperium.

But I could still see Holloway wheezing, slumped against the wall.

With the last of my strength, I looked up and saw Irene Adler – Adler-Bot -- looking down at me, a grin at the corner of her mouth.

She turned from me and jammed the data spike into the main console.

In my earpiece, Miriam kept me updated as she data-dumped everything:

The evidence, the witnesses, the crackdown, the plan for mass Morlock deportation and labor camp relocation to benefit the Ascendancy, every last dirty secret.

Even that stupid dialogue about eliminating ethnic food eaters.

The feed went live, streaming across every channel.

Maximum distribution.

I saw Holloway try to claw towards me, but his strength was gone.

A shot rang out — one of the IC enforcers I'd laid out wasn't quite as down for the count as I'd hoped, apparently.

I felt the sting of the bullet, sharp, in my chest. It suddenly became much harder to breathe.

Adler-Bot pulled a pistol from a shoulder holster, and – appropriately enough -- shot the enforcer in his face, which exploded into a red puddle as his brains burst out the back of his skull.

Naughty Adler-Bot, I thought, you aren't using frangible rounds either.

I assumed I was as good as dead, but at least the job was done. Now we just had to hope the data dump would inspire someone with authority to do *something*.

I could no longer raise my head. I could feel my body getting cold and numb.

I watched as the screens flickered above the console and a thousand voices screamed at once.

Then Adler-Bot was above me and sticking a needle into my neck.

As whatever was in the syringe entered my system and I started to black out, Miriam's voice was the last thing I heard, talking to me gently through my earpiece:

"You did good, Kestrel."

Weakly, I smiled.

"That's the first time you've called me that," I croaked.

As everything went dark, I said a silent prayer that she was right.

Chapter Forty

I woke up in a med bay, Superintendent Constable Bilbo Brannigan standing over me.

"Don't tell me," I said, my voice hoarse. "I've died and gone to *Gehenna*."

Gehenna, by the way, is the Jewish version of hell.

(Insert corny mother-in-law joke here.)

Brannigan scoffed. "I don't know where this *Gehenna* place is, but you're still alive, despite your best efforts, and much to the chagrin of a great many in the Imperium."

"Including you?"

Brannigan grinned. "I'm surprised at you," he said. "Haven't you figured out by now I don't give a toss if you live or die?"

I swallowed, my throat parched, spittle going down hard like a lump. "Ok," I said. "So, why *am* I still alive?"

"Someone in the Intelligencer Service sifted through your Imperium-wide data dump and didn't like it what it added up to."

"The Royal Nixonian Galactic Imperial Intelligencer Service objected to the Ascendancy plans for the Belt?" I asked, incredulous. "The Intelligencer Service is nothing but Imperial loyalty police."

"True enough, but they decided the data you dumped showed that the Ascendancy is not quite sufficiently loyal to the Imperium for their tastes . . . . or for the Imperator's. Too much tail wagging the dog with those Space Nazis. The Imperator will tolerate any amount of cruelty and malfeasance to Morlocks in service to his rule, but he won't tolerate disloyalty to himself personally or his Imperium generally. He doesn't like anyone else's tail wagging *his* dog. The Ascendancy wanted to put their blood purity ideology above allegiance to Nixonianism and, worse, above allegiance to Richard II himself . . . and that simply won't do."

"So, what happened while I was out?"

"Before the purge of Morlocks got fully underway, the Belt was flooded with Special Boat Service Cockleshell Commando units, who rounded up the Ascendancy militias and are now interrogating corporate security and administration as well as the whole of Fort Checkers personnel *and* the Ministry of Internal Compliance and the Ministry of Ancestral Heritage and Pickleball, in addition to upper management of Heliotrope and the *Mensch-Machine Volk-Roboter* corporation, trying to sort the traitors from the loyalists. Holloway and a few thousand others at the top of those organizations are already floating in the void, along with every one of their minions that got one of those neural receptor implants that made the Wagner Prime arias into ecstatic religious-slash-political loyalty experiences for them."

"They spaced them?" I asked. "All of them?"

"That's what the Imperium does to traitors," Brannigan said. "More are likely to follow. People are already taking bets. The smart money's on a purge of tens of thousands, but some put the final toll into the millions. It's ten to one against a billion, but it's not out of the question in an empire of trillions of souls. We'll have to see how the investigation works out."

I sighed. "So, we stopped a purge of Morlocks and began a purge of Ascendancy?" I said.

Brannigan laughed. "You did, lad, you did at that," he said. "Sure, but what else did you expect?"

"I was hoping not to be complicit in mass murder, at a minimum."

Brannigan laughed again, harder and less laughingly. "You fought in the War of the Southern Sky lad. A trillion dead in that before it was all over. What was that if not mass murder?"

He had a point.

There didn't seem to be much to be gained in dwelling on my personal culpability in mass murder.

I was hardly alone in that in this galaxy.

"What's happened to Wagner Prime?" I asked.

"The techs are trying to delete him across all the systems, but he's a slippery bugger, that one. And since he's made of pixels and algorithms instead of flesh and blood, his ghost may live on in the machine long after his original code has been deleted."

"And they still don't know who was really behind it all," I said. "I mean, the ones at the top of the food chain."

"Those people are never held accountable, Kestenbaum. You're a smart boy. You've read the history books. They just change uniforms and find a new ideology in which to insert their toxic philosophies. The galaxy spirals on, and they spiral along with it until the next reckoning."

"You make me wish I hadn't survived the gunshots," I said.

"You and half the Imperium," Brannigan said. "But you've got a few admirers among the *hoi polloi*. Don't knock it. *My* only admirer is my bartender and that's only because I always pay me tab on time."

Brannigan left, and I dozed off.

When I awoke, Miriam and Adler-Bot were standing at my bedside.

"I didn't know you two knew each other," I said.

"We've both applied for and been granted full personhood," Miriam said. "We proved our full sentience and sapience."

Adler-Bot smiled and took Miriam's hand. "Also, we're girlfriends."

I narrowed my eyes. "By which you mean, you're not girls who are friends, but . . ."

Miriam and Adler-Bot smiled and looked at each other deeply with an expression that strongly resembled affection. They kissed one another on the mouth, lovingly.

"Not girls who are friends, no," Miriam said.

"Proper girlfriends," Adler-Bot said.

And they kissed again.

"Well," I said. "My best to you both."

Miriam scowled at me. "Why didn't you tell me I snored?" she said.

"I assumed you knew already."

Miriam looked affronted. "I didn't. Adler-Bot informed me. I have now downloaded a patch to eliminate that aspect of my programming."

"Don't eliminate it," Adler-Bot said. "I quite like it. I find it terribly cute."

Miriam scrutinized Adler-Bot for a moment, to see if she was sincere.

"I have now deleted the patch," Miriam announced.

Chapter Forty-one

In the dead of night, I awoke to the sound of a robot reciting a Hebrew prayer at my bedside.

In my half-sleeping state, I mistook if for the Kaddish, the Jewish prayer for the dead.

"Well, hell," I said. "I guess I didn't make it after all."

The robotic voice kept reciting, and as I regained full wakefulness, I soon realized it wasn't the Kaddish after all, but the *Mi Shebeirach* – the Jewish prayer for healing.

As my eyes adjusted to the dark, I saw the voice belonged to Eliyahu-Bot.

"Thank you," I said when the prayer finished. "I'm sure I can use all the help I can get."

"Where does the lawman go after he triumphs over his own overlords?" he replied.

"There you go with that cryptic bull crap again," I said. "But I'm going back to the Reach."

"Not where your body goes, lawman," he said. "Where goes your soul?"

"Where goes yours?" I asked. "What is your *shtick*, exactly?"

"No *shtick*," he said. "Only *emet*."

"*Emet*" is Hebrew for "truth."

I was feeling exhausted by his inability to be straightforward. "Well, I'm going back to sleep, Rabbi Robot," I said. "Thank you for stopping by."

I lay back down in the hospital bed and rolled over on my side.

I lay there, eyes closed, but listening to his diodes hum for a while as he watched over me.

Then I listen to his gears whir as he left the room.

I lay awake for a few moments longer, listening to make

certain he had really left.

When at last convinced that he had, I allowed myself to drift back to sleep.

I dreamed of robots with angel wings singing in a heavenly choir.

They sang Anthropocene Epoch Jewish singer/songwriter Leonard Cohen's famous song, "Hallelujah."

Go figure.

Chapter Forty-two

I awoke with a start and found myself staring into a bright light in my otherwise dark hospital room.

"Yonah Kestenbaum, the Enemies List Liberation Front accuses you of settler-colonial enforcement and of acting as a proxy for the tyranny of the Imperium," said a voice.

I sat up in my bed and blinked, trying to see who was accusing me. As my eyes adjusted, I saw two young people, a man and a woman, maybe twenty years of age, each.

They looked more like college students than Morlocks. They could have been Medii, or even Patrician. ELLF had long appealed to the disaffected from all walks of life.

In any case, these two were clearly cosplaying hipster radicalism – which did not mean they weren't dangerous.

"I'm afraid you'll have to be more specific," I said.

"You've spent your entire adult life in service to the tyrannical Imperium," they said.

"Are you guys students?" I said. "There isn't a university in the galaxy that isn't accountable to the same tyrannical Imperium."

"You fought for ten years in the colonial War of the Southern Sky," the young woman said.

"That was to repel an invasion force that arrived through the Sagittarius A black hole at the center of our galaxy," I reminded them. "We still don't know where they came from or where they returned to. *They* were clearly the colonists. Besides, I was drafted, as were most of the Imperial fighters. You probably don't know this because you weren't yet born."

"You have recently thwarted an ELLF attack aimed at the heart of Imperial Morlock oppression and industrial production in the interests of the ruling class."

"I think even you two know that's not true," I said. "ELLF had nothing to with this recent unpleasantness. Although I can see why ELLF would be jealous."

They ignored me and pressed on. They took turns reading to me from a prepared "indictment."

It went like this:

ENEMIES LIST LIBERATION FRONT (ELLF): PROCLAMATION OF INDICTMENT

Concerning the Individual Known as Marshal Yonah Kestenbaum

To the Dispossessed Peoples of the Reach, To the Morlock multitudes, the indentured, the erased, the uncounted —

WHEREAS the so-called Royal Nixonian Galactic Imperium maintains its dominion through violence masked as order, law disguised as inevitability, and "peace" enforced at the barrel of a sanctioned weapon;

WHEREAS its marshals serve not as guardians of justice but as instruments of settler-colonial expansion, pacifying the frontier so that extraction may proceed unimpeded;

WHEREAS one Yonah Kestenbaum, bearing the title of Deputy Marshal, has knowingly and repeatedly acted in service of this machinery of domination;

WHEREAS Yonah Kestenbaum is a member of a race of settler-colonists, apartheiders, ZioNazis, war-criminals, genociders, Rootless Cosmopolitans, and terrorists created by the

Rothschilds of Old Earth 19th century;

WE HEREBY INDICT HIM.

ON THE FIRST COUNT:
That he has enforced the edicts of a distant throne upon peoples who neither consent to nor benefit from its rule;

ON THE SECOND COUNT:
That he has hunted, detained, and neutralized those who resist dispossession, branding them criminals so that their grievances may be dismissed and their suffering rendered invisible;

ON THE THIRD COUNT:
That he has lent the legitimacy of his person — his origin among the marginalized, his fluency in the languages of the oppressed — to the very system that consumes them;

ON THE FOURTH COUNT:
That he has, by action and reputation alike, made occupation appear tolerable, thereby deepening its hold;

ON THE FIFTH COUNT:
That he did knowingly and deliberately shoot corporate overlord Tiger Halden in the face in order to claim for himself a deceptive status as a protector of the oppressed and enemy of the oppressor;

AND ON THE FINAL, MOST GRIEVOUS COUNT:

*That in dismantling the recent operation of the
so-called Ascendancy, he has deprived the
peoples of the galaxy of a moment of
unmasking —
a moment in which the naked logic of
domination might have stood revealed to all —
a moment in which the indifferent cruelty of
empire and its rivals might have burned so
brightly that even the willfully blind could no
longer look away.*

*We condemn the theft of this revelation, for it is
in crisis that systems expose themselves. It is
in catastrophe that the lie collapses. And in
denying that catastrophe, the Marshal has
preserved the illusion.*

*He has prolonged the dream.
He has perpetuated the nightmare.*

THEREFORE:

*Let no one claim ignorance.
Let no one say the machinery is hidden.*

*It is visible — in the badge he carries, in the
warrants he executes, in the silence that
follows his passing.*

WE DECLARE:

*That Yonah Kestenbaum is not merely a
functionary, but an active, willing, and
enthusiastic collaborator in the maintenance of
a violent order;*

*That his actions, however justified in the
language of "stability" or "necessity," serve
only to extend the life of a system already in
moral bankruptcy and decline;*

*That the frontier he patrols is not lawless, but
unlawfully colonized;*

AND WE PROCLAIM:

*That no badge sanctifies injustice.
That no law redeems dispossession.
That no act of "heroism" excuses the
preservation of a dying tyranny.*

LET THIS STAND AS NOTICE:

*To the Marshal —
we see you.*

*To those who would follow him —
we name you.*

*To those who believe the system can be
reformed from within —
we warn you.*

*The ledger is long.
The reckoning is patient.*

And the illusion will not hold forever.

"For these and other crimes we find you guilty and
sentence you to die," they concluded. "Please read this
statement as we prepare to behead you."

They paused a moment to let that sink in.

"Ok, in the first place, I didn't shoot Tiger Halden in the face," I said.

"Everyone saw the vid," the girl said.

"In the second place, basically you're telling me that ELLF is sad that I stopped a massive deportation and enslavement of ninety trillion Morlocks because you wanted to use that to feed your propaganda engine. I mean, come on, guys, you totally suck."

"Read this," the girl said, as the boy handed me the piece of paper upon which were written the words: *"For these and all other crimes for which I am accused, I plead guilty and accept the consequences of my actions."*

I looked up from the paper. "You're kidding right? No way am I going to read that."

"We will behead you either way," said the young man, as he pulled a machete from the sheath on his belt.

That was when a figure rose out of nowhere behind them and cracked both their heads together with the alarmingly loud sound of two coconuts crashing into one another.

Both kids dropped like sandbags.

Berek stood in their place.

"In the name of Nixon's toenail clippings, Berek, did you kill them?" I asked.

Berek looked down at them on the floor. "This one is still breathing," he said. "I think."

I sighed. "To what do I owe the pleasure of your company, Berek?" I asked.

"Just stopped by to save your life," he said, then added, cheekily: "Again."

He had saved my life more than once during the war, but in fairness, I had saved his more than once as well.

"I'm going to press the button to call in the nurse," I said. "You'd better make yourself scarce."

Berek smiled. "*Shalom,*" he said and slipped out the door almost noiselessly.

I waited a moment and then pressed the button, wondering how I was going to explain all this to the nurse on duty.

231

Chapter Forty-three

I was in the med bay for ten days as I recovered.

Brannigan came to visit me occasionally, bringing a flask of Betelgeuse whiskey to share.

Miriam and Adler-Bot stopped by as well, replaying newsfeed reports of the data dump and the events in the Belt.

The newsfeeds downplayed the extent of the Ascendancy treachery and painted me as a stumblebum who accidentally blundered into the truth and subsequently had to be rescued by the Imperial Intelligencer Service and the Cockleshell Commandos.

Which, I had to admit, was basically true. Assuming Adler-Bot was really an Intelligencer-bot.

In any case, no matter what she was, Irene Adler-Bot was top of the heap, in my humble estimation.

After ten days, I was discharged from the med bay.

I climbed aboard a transport shuttle back to Orin's World, with Miriam, who insisted she still wanted to work as my deputy, even though I assured her she was free to follow other pursuits. Adler-Bot joined us. She wasn't certain as to what was next for her professionally, she said.

Come to think of it, I still wasn't really completely certain for whom she was working in the first place.

I sat by a window. Miriam and Adler-Bot sat behind me, where they commenced to cuddle and make out and giggle like schoolgirls.

That's when Hadar Ruan slipped into the seat behind me.

I looked at her and couldn't resist a smile. "I thought you'd skipped town," I said.

"I was busy," she said. "In all the chaos, and with all the scrutiny, we forced the corporation to recognize the Assembly and negotiate a contract. It's not perfect, but it's a hell of a lot better than before."

"Every crisis is an opportunity," I said. "At least for someone. Give me the highlights."

"Free medical care, free housing, free food, debts wiped clean, no more indebtedness for using tools and equipment supplied by the corporation, no more fees for oxygen or water or taking up space, better living conditions, no more decades-long unbreakable contracts, better wages, workplace safety rules, better working conditions and regulated working hours, and a Heliotrope-Assembly dispute resolution board. Also, free Heliotrope ice cream. The real thing. Not the soya-based kind."

"I'm most surprised about the ice cream," I admitted.

"Me too," Hadar said, delightedly. "We just sort of threw it in there to see what they'd do."

"Are you going on to the next stop to organize the Morlocks?"

"Yes," she said. "We've got a lot of organizing still to do, and we still anticipate that at some point we'll need to call a general strike to really establish Morlock labor and personhood rights under Imperial law."

"Sounds like a tall order."

"It will be. But I have ten days to kill before I get started." She smiled at me and took my hand. "I was hoping you'd help me kill them, Kestrel."

I didn't have words to respond to that, so I leaned into Hadar and we kissed.

That seemed to be response enough.

The data dump continued to spread throughout the Imperium, and even beyond. The Imperium continued to spin the story, making it about an insufficiently loyal faction within the empire, rather than a mass deportation-mass incarceration-mass labor enslavement movement with its tentacles deep within the centers of Imperial power and which would likely take years to fully unwind.

But the truth — the full truth, the actual truth — was there, too, if you knew where to look.

In the Rim bars and the Morlock dens, people told the story different. They said I'd punched a hole in the sun-wheel, left a scar on the propaganda so deep even the next purge wouldn't wipe it away.

Sometimes, in the quiet hours, you could even hear the old songs, remixed and raw, sometimes even with my name buried in the backbeat.

But it wasn't all about me, of course.

Heroes are fine, but in the end, it's not heroes but peoples, movements, and organizing that makes the difference.

That and, I guess, avoiding infighting between anarcho-syndicalists and anarcho-communists.

The Morlocks weren't there yet. I wouldn't exactly say they were really close, either.

But they were closer than they'd been.

And that wasn't nothing.

It had come at a terrible cost in lives. One hundred thousand people were spaced by the Imperium in the aftermath, most of them guilty as hell, but some of them only marginally so.

But if the needle had moved in the other direction, the cost would have been higher, and the body count much greater, involving other people entirely. More innocent people.

The people who did get punished and shoved out an airlock weren't those at the very top of the Space Nazi pyramid. Those kind of people are rarely punished.

But they weren't exactly innocent, either.

Like that Old Anthropocene Epoch song: "No One Is Innocent."

And as far as I can tell, no one is. Including me.

But some of us are less innocent than others.

As for me, I was going back to my marshal office.

I had to admit, buried in the lunacy, the ELLF indictment against me did have a few good points.

But I would continue to try to uphold the law without perpetuating tyranny as best I could. Not an easy balance to strike in the Royal Nixonian Galactic Imperium. But it fell on me to continue to try to strike it, at least in the Reach.

And the Reach, after all was said and done, was once again my home.

The End

ABOUT THE AUTHOR

Peter Ullian is the author of the novels *The Last Electric House* and *The Republic of Broken Places,* both from Swamp Angel Press. His full-length collection of short stories, *Pulp & Circumstance,* made the Amazon bestseller lists in the categories of "Historical Fiction Short Stories" and "Jewish Historical Fiction." The 2019-2020 Poet Laureate of Beacon, New York, his poetry has been published in anthologies and periodicals and collected in *The Fevered-Dream Crimes of Pulp-Fiction Poets and Other Love Stories: New and Collected Poems* (Lion in Autumn Music Publishing), and the chapbook *Secret Histories* & Exobiologies (Poet's Haven). His short stories have been published in *Cemetery Dance Magazine, Frontier Tales Magazine,* and the DAW Books Anthology *Star Colonies.* His work for the stage has been produced off-Broadway, regionally, and internationally, and directed by theatre artists such as Harold Prince. His work has been nominated for the Pushcart Prize and the Rhysling Award. He has received awards from the Kennedy Center and production grants from the National Endowment for the Arts. He lives in New York's Hudson Valley with his family.

www.ingramcontent.com/pod-product-compliance
Lightning Source LLC
Chambersburg PA
CBHW051507030726
47592CB00006B/2133